Angel's Collar

Love Strictly Tested Book One

by

Anna Hague

Angel's Collar

Contact Information: info@thewildrosepress.com

Cover Art by *Diana Carlile*

The Wild Rose Press, Inc.
PO Box 708
Adams Basin, NY 14410-0708

Visit us at www.thewilderroses.com

Publishing History
First Scarlet Rose Edition, 2018
Print ISBN 978-1-5092-1986-5
Digital ISBN 978-1-5092-1985-8

Published in the United States of America

Learning the ropes isn't easy.

"Oh my gosh," I squealed. My hand barely covered the gaping hole my mouth formed. "I am so sorry."

The massive red wine stain all over the front of a pure white shirt on a rock hard chest glared like a traffic light. As my gaze traveled up and up, his face, in addition to being a visual perfection, appeared rather amused. Well, at least that's what I deducted while devouring those ice blue eyes which complemented the thick rich brown hair which was a little too long for a guy in a fancy suit. Chocolate lava cake at its best. All I wanted to do was to swirl whipped cream all over this sinful dessert of a man.

"Here, let me get some club soda and towels." I wanted to make a quick retreat to find a way to repair the damage to his shirt as well as my embarrassment.

"No. Don't worry. It's all right." He regarded the stain and then me. "You could have just introduced yourself instead of ruining my shirt."

"Well. I do like to make an impression." His genuine smile made me relax and I felt too warm all over. "Really, though, let me pay for the cleaning."

"It's just a shirt." He crossed his arms over his chest. "I'm still waiting."

"For…" I was confused, befuddled, and hopelessly embarrassed.

"An introduction."

Wow. He was serious about knowing who I was. "I'm Emma Samuelson." I couldn't decide whether to extend my hand, kneel at his expensive Italian shoes, or just bat my eyes to flirt.

I'm a terrible flirt, and by terrible I mean, I do it often, but not all that well, and kneeling would draw attention. So, I extended my sweaty hand.

Dedication

To the Indiana Romance Writers of America.
Never have I been a part of such a supportive group.
Thank you. To my fantastically supportive husband.
You're my everything.

Chapter One

I know my husband could tell I was nervous. Even after the short time we'd been married, he grasped every subtle change and nuance my body projected. Rarely, could I hide anything or any emotion.

"Emma, come here." He held out his arms to me. I'm not fond of the name Emma. I had a six-hundred-year-old Aunt Emma, and she smelled. What a namesake.

I stepped into his arms, feeling the heat from his chest and a slight increase in pressure from his crotch. "Not now," I whispered.

"Maybe a little poke could ease some of your nerves," he teased.

"I think poking would only make things worse." I attempted to make some daylight between our burgeoning arousals. "Besides, she'll be here any minute."

"You don't have to do this." He rubbed my arms, only displacing the hair standing on end for an immeasurable number of seconds. "Call her and tell her you've changed your mind."

"Part of me wants to call and cancel, but I just feel this is something I should do. I know I'm not the only one who wants to talk."

"No, you're not," He whispered in my ear before brushing his lips against mine. I shivered from the simple gesture of love and the scruff from his face raking across my skin. Maybe a little poke might be a good idea.

Scruff—something so different from the smooth skin of the clean-shaven face I remembered.

"I'm more nervous about this," I said pointing to my head, "And slipping up, making a mistake. I don't want to blow to our cover." Even in Indianapolis, you still run into people you know.

He fingered one of my long coppery tendrils before giving it a gentle tug. "Emma, this wig cost a fortune. If I weren't already aware, I'd never know this wasn't your real hair. With those green contacts, she won't be able to tell your eyes are blue. And those glasses just add to your disguise. Just remember, if you stutter about anything, a good reporter will know you're lying."

He backed me against the taupe-colored wall of the suite and raised my hands high over my head, pinning them to the wall. "I just hope she's an ethical reporter or we're screwed."

His hands slipped under the fold of my cashmere camel-colored turtleneck and fingered the leather collar beneath the neck of the sweater. I wore several different collars for different reasons and occasions. I had one we reserved for fancy social functions. It passed as expensive jewelry and no one was the wiser.

I didn't wear this particular collar on a day-to-day basis, but rather only certain times. However, for my impending endeavor, I wanted something that shouted my choice to live an *alternative* lifestyle.

Sounds weird, but the feel and sometimes the rigidity gave me a sense of calm and peace. I understood where and to whom I belonged. And when I say *belonged,* I mean in my heart.

But right now, my nerves drove the snug feeling too tight, and not in a good way.

The reporter was coming to this hotel suite to interview me about my life choice, wearing a collar for my husband. Still, it's hard for me to say I'm a submissive. Well, I mean I am, but not always. I was…well, complicated was an understatement. Hell, this life had been complicated for me to understand and embrace.

I'd replied to the reporter's call out to women living in unusual and non-traditional marriages. I used a pre-paid phone when we talked. No way did I want a trace back to my real cell phone, nor did I leave any electronic trail with e-mail. We called and texted to set up this interview in the suite of the best hotel in the city, close to my husband's work and just blocks from our home in the city. Staring out of the window of this glass structure hotel, I caught a glimpse of our home in the distance.

Jessica Forner was going to tell my story. According to her, she would be open, fair, and non-judgmental. I hoped her promise rang true. Though in the beginning, I had major problems with the kink life. Now, I had accepted and embraced this life so much so, I'm not sure I could live any other way.

I know I can't.

Even now, waiting for Jessica to arrive, visions of what my husband does to me in our home, on a chair, on the counter, our bed, and pretty much anywhere, impeded my ability to stand.

A knock on the door startled me back to the

present. He smiled at my flinch and subsequent shiver and added a kiss to my forehead to send me on my way. "It'll be fine, and when you're finished, we'll make use of this suite, which is also costing me a fortune."

He might have a terrific job, but he followed every penny.

"Oh, wait a sec." He stopped me. "Your ring?"

I studied my wedding set. The princess cut diamond sparkled with the sunlight coming from the window. Eight smaller diamonds circled the engagement ring while my gold band sported two rows of small diamonds. I think he blew the rule of thumb about two month's salary should be the norm for an engagement ring out of the window for this set, but I never asked. I didn't want to know. I also didn't want to remove my rings. I never had before and was reluctant to do so now.

"But?"

Always practical, my husband said. "The rings could be another way of identifying you."

A cold chill gripped me as I slipped off the rings, handing them to his outstretched hands. "You're right."

I looked at the indentation on my finger. "This feels wrong."

He cupped my chin, forcing my gaze up, way up to meet his eyes. "It's not for long and for good reason only. Otherwise, I would never ask you or even let you take those off."

I shut the bedroom door, hearing the lock turn behind me, and started the trek to meet in person the woman I'd only known from text messages. We had never met in person, so for all I knew, she could be in disguise, but I doubted any reporter would use a disguise. They all wanted notoriety. She requested her boyfriend accompany her to the interview. I declined, telling her I preferred to talk exclusively between the two of us, and if she had fears about this, he could wait in the lobby, and she could call him if she became anxious with anything I said.

I'm not sure what her fears were, maybe she anticipated we would try to kidnap her to sell her into sexual slavery. I think such a belief might be a common opinion of those who didn't understand a BDSM life style choice.

I opened the door to a twenty-something pale-skinned woman with shiny black hair. She carried a messenger-style bag slung over lightweight jacket, perfect for the March dampness.

"Jessica?"

"Yes," she hesitated, "You're my interview, Angel?"

Initially, I used the old nickname. We kept all correspondence to a first-name only relationship, and I told her I'd likely pick aliases for the story. I'm not ashamed of my choice now, but life would be difficult for everyone if people learned how we lived. No one wants to be ostracized or be seen as a freak.

"Come in. Let's sit over here." I pointed to the love seat and sofa that mirrored each other in the suite's living area. We made our way toward the modern, but comfortable tan furniture. "Would you like something to drink?"

"Ah, maybe some water is all." She dropped her bag on the loveseat, unzipped her jacket, and sat down.

I retrieved two bottles of water from the suite's small fridge. I handed her one as I sat on the sofa to face her.

"Thanks." She set the bottle on the table between us, before producing a small tape recorder and her laptop.

My nerves panicked. "I'd prefer you not use a tape recorder." Voice recognition, you know.

"Oh, Okay. Then could I take notes on my laptop? Writing by hand isn't really easy for me anymore since I use the computer so much."

"That's fine," I said. "Just no recording."

"Sure thing. Can we start?" Jessica asked.

Okay. I'm a little nervous," I admitted. Little might be the understatement of the year. I was about to pee myself.

"You and me both." She smiled. A nail-bitten finger pointed to my neck. "Can I see?"

I nodded and gathered the sweater over my head, praying I had secured the wig with enough pins. Underneath, I wore a white cotton tank top. In fact, my nerves had made me hot and uncomfortable in the sweater.

I lay the sweater aside, and when I looked up, I could see Jessica's wide-eyed reaction to the leather collar encompassing my neck. My husband always said I had a beautiful long neck, so what I was wearing was not even close to covering my neck, but I had one we used on occasion.

I didn't know what to say yet, so I just gave a little smile.

She was shocked or mesmerized or both. I couldn't tell. After an uneasy silence, she spoke.

"May I touch it?" she asked.

"Sure. It won't jump off and attach itself to you," I

teased.

She laughed with a nervous tone. Ice broken I hoped.

With a tentative motion of a deer, Jessica sat next to me on the sofa. With tremendous hesitation, she put her right hand's fingers to my collar, touching the soft pliable leather, not at all stiff like one I had. I didn't want to scare her any more than she appeared to be.

That one rather scared me or pissed me off, or both, and much to my husband's delight.

Her icy finger almost hooked inside. She was trying to feel how tight my collar was. The leather gave, but not much and, she yanked away her hand.

I understood. "It's not as tight as you think," I assured her. "Just one of the things you get used to."

"I'm sorry," she apologized. "I said I wouldn't judge, and I won't. It's just very odd to me."

I smiled at her explanation. I saw myself in her answer. "It was very odd to me at first and for a while, but now…this symbol is so much a part of me."

She returned to the love seat and twisted the cap from the water bottle, taking a long drink before she opened the laptop. Like me, I bet she wished the water were alcohol.

"Can we get started? How about at the beginning, before this." She pointed to the collar.

"Okay. Like I said before on the phone. I will be very honest and graphic."

"That's what I want." Suddenly, Jessica acted more like a journalist than the nervous girl who just fingered my neck.

I began a story I couldn't afford to screw up.

"How it all started was…"

Chapter Two

"Oh my gosh," I squealed. My hand barely covered the gaping hole my mouth formed. "I am so sorry." The massive red wine stain all over the front of a pure white shirt on a rock hard chest glared like a traffic light. As my gaze traveled up and up, his face, in addition to being a visual perfection, appeared rather amused. Well, at least that's what I deducted, while devouring those ice blue eyes which complemented the thick rich brown hair which was a little too long for a guy in a fancy suit. Chocolate lava cake at its best. All I wanted to do was to swirl whipped cream all over this sinful dessert of a man.

"Here, let me get some club soda and towels." I wanted to make a quick retreat to find a way to repair the damage to his shirt as well as my embarrassment.

"No. Don't worry. It's all right." He regarded the stain and then me. "You could have just introduced yourself instead of ruining my shirt."

"Well. I do like to make an impression." His genuine smile made me relax and too warm all over. "Really, though, let me pay for the cleaning."

"It's just a shirt." He crossed his arms over his chest. "I'm still waiting."

"Forrrr?" I was confused, befuddled, and hopelessly embarrassed.

"An introduction."

Wow. He was serious about knowing who I was. "I'm Emma Samuelson." I couldn't decide whether to extend my hand, kneel at his expensive Italian shoes, or just bat my eyes to flirt.

I'm a terrible flirt, and by terrible I mean, I do it often, but not all that well, and kneeling would draw attention. So, I extended my sweaty hand.

"Emma." He enunciated each syllable. I was positive he did so he'd place my face with the name and remember to steer clear. "What a lovely name."

I think my toes curled. "Thank you. Although, I've never been too thrilled with my name. It's a family name."

"Well, Emma suits you. A pure and traditional name for a memorable woman."

Could he see me getting red? I blushed like an apple ready to pick. Okay. Let's change the subject. "And you are?"

"Jordan Caldera. He gripped my hand tighter. "Nice to meet you, Emma Samuelson."

Jordan Caldera. Just the sound of his name sent a message all of the way down to my happy place. Even his name was hot.

As the warmth of his hand in mine ignited, I know my red turned crimson, but I covered my reaction well, at least I believed so. "Nice to meet you, Jordan Caldera. I should get back to my group. They are the ones putting on this fundraiser. I just tagged along. I'm nobody, really." Nice ramble. "Again, I should pay you for the cleaning bill for your shirt."

He still had my hand as I broke hold. I fixated on our clasped hands and so did he. Might have been my over eager imagination, but I confidently speculated him reluctant to break the connection.

"I'll let you know." He kept smiling, but I turned to walk away with any remnants of dignity I had left. Who am I kidding? I had none.

I walked away an ungraceful, tragic embarrassed idiot across the room to join my friends who were actually only acquaintances I managed to charm for entrance to this affair: Sara, Finn, Lilly, and Stewart. Sara and Finn were the chairpersons of the Books to All campaign. Lilly and Stewart were handling the PR, and I pretended to have some knowledge of high-end fundraisers. What I did for a living was edit teen fiction novels. I swear if I had to read one more book about dystopic societies where teens have to escape from the lion's den to survive, I was relatively sure I would, with no reservations, offer myself up to the lion.

The rest of the evening, I found myself glancing around the hotel ballroom. All right, not glancing in the least. I was searching for ice blue eyes on a face taller than most every other man in the room was.

Every now and then, I would catch a glance of him in conversation with other attendees. His height made him easy to spot. Once, he caught me staring and smiled, acknowledging my ogling. Again embarrassed, I promised myself no more room scanning and concentrated on whoever was standing right in front of me, regardless of how much shrimp cocktail sauce dripped down his shirt.

Thank God the band fired up, and the background music helped me relax a little. Just as I almost let go of the disaster of spilling red wine on the hottest guy in the room, I flinched from an instant heat touching my elbow. When I turned around, Jordan—I loved saying his name—was so close, our bodies nearly collided. The turning in my stomach either signaled food poisoning or an extreme attraction. I think it was the latter.

"No drink?" He pointed to my empty hand, brushing the tips of my fingers.

Still embarrassed at my fifth-grade crush imitation, I searched for the right words, and yes, your brain can hurt from thinking up something witty.

"I have a limited budget for cleaning, so I should cut back on potential calamities."

He laughed at my self-deprecation. "In that case, would you care to dance with me?"

The song the band was playing was slow and required no particular skill, but I hesitated. "I'm sorry. I'm not much of a dancer."

He clasped my hand, leading me toward the dance floor. "Neither am I."

I think he was lying about the dancing. He pulled me close enough I could smell the wine on his shirt as he controlled the dance in my favor. "You're making me appear to have rhythm," I said.

"You don't need any help there." I heard a slightly exasperated sigh from high above. "Are you going to continue to stare at the stain on my shirt?"

I wasn't watching his face because the rising and falling of his chest mesmerized me. "Well, in my defense, considering you are at least a foot taller than I am, that's kinda where my eye level is."

His hand shifted from around my waist to my chin. "You could look at me instead of me having to stare at the top of your head, even though the top of your head is pretty fine."

11

My knees almost buckled. His arm snaked around my waist. "You okay?"

"Just dandy." *Shit. I didn't just say that, did I?*

As the music ended, I released my hold on his shoulder, but he did not release me. "Thank you, Emma, for dancing with me and ruining my shirt. I need to leave, but I was wondering if we could see each other another time. I would like to spend some time with you in a less formal situation."

Stunned he was interested in anything beyond our flirtatious exchanges, I had difficulty forming any coherent words. "I, ah, well, ah; I maybe, yes, well, maybe, well, possibly…"

"Is there an answer in there somewhere?"

Deep breath. "Yes. Yes. I would like to spend some time with you." My inability to think gave him enough time to reconsider.

"Emma?"

"Yes?"

"In order for this to happen, I'm going to need your phone number," he said.

"I'm sorry. You may regret ever asking me out. My phone is there." I pointed to one of the round tables near the stage. We walked to the table, and I retrieved my phone from my purse. "If you tell me your number, I'll send you a text. That way you will always have it. Unless you delete me, which I would completely understand if you did."

"My phone number is: 317-555-1212," he rattled off. "I won't delete you."

"I won't call you, excessively, like a stalker or anything."

"Good to know. Good night, Emma Samuelson.

You have made a rather dull evening quite the event."

Speechless, I drooled as he walked away through the ballroom exit.

Oh dear God the view's just as good from the back.

When I returned to my group, I first turned around to make sure he'd left the room, and then I did a happy dance impressive enough for any judge on *Dancing With the Stars*.

"Who the hell was that?" Lilly grabbed my upper arm. "I don't know this guy. I thought I knew most everyone here."

I began taping my knuckles for an ugly wave of catfight. I flunked sharing in kindergarten.

"Stay away. I spilled wine on him first. His name is Jordan Caldera, and he just asked me out." I stuck out my adult tongue.

Finn raised a finger. "Oh. I know who he is. He's some guy from…I don't know…that big firm here in town."

"Well, that was helpful," I said.

"You didn't even ask what he did?" Finn's eye roll did nothing to squash my amazing good mood.

"I wasn't really interested in what he did. Quite honestly, a guy who walks around looking like sex in a suit can do anything he wants. I just want him to include me."

"Someone has a bad case of the hots." Lilly kissed my cheek. "Well I hope your date goes well."

I flared my arms and bowed to my friends. "Thank you. I've got to go."

"You mean you want to go call Sabrina." Finn waved good-bye as I turned to the exit.

"It's required. She's my bestie."

Anna Hague

As soon as the valet fetched my car, and I stepped outside, I speed dialed my best friend Sabrina. Since the third grade, Sabrina was my personal diary, noting every entry with enthusiasm, love, and sometimes criticism.

"Pick up. Pick up," I begged while trying to maneuver my way through downtown Friday night traffic.

"Hey Jaynie. How was the big party?" She always called me by my middle name. Another name I held little regard for.

"Well," I attempted to sound blasé. "You know, shrimp cocktail, cheese, mediocre band, stuffy people, but...one part was fucking fabulous!"

"What's his name?" Years of friendship inclined to expose shallow tendencies.

"Jordan Caldera."

"Damn. His name sounds fuckin' orgasmic," she said. "So, how did you meet?"

Interesting choice of words coming from a girl whose mother told her she'd go to Hell for cussing and a girl who'd had sex only a handful of times.

If I lied and said our eyes met across the room, and he bee-lined over and asked me out, Sabrina would say "liar," and hang up. "I spilled a glass of red wine all over his white shirt."

"That's my girl!" She squealed.

"He wasn't even upset about me ruining what was I'm sure an expensive shirt. Then later, he asked me to dance. Then, he said he had to leave, but he asked me for my number, and a date. I was like, 'Oh my fuckin' God'."

"Super exciting," Sabrina said. "What's he look

14

like? Not because looks matter, but yeah, they matter."

"Indeed, the best part of all. He's the human equivalent of the male models we drool over in magazines. Very classy. Veeerrrrry tall. His hair is this deep dark chocolate, like expensive chocolate. A little longer, but not real long, but the front kinda flops over his forehead. He's super sexy. I was so shocked he asked me out."

"Oh come on. Jaynie. He wouldn't have asked you out if he didn't think you were awesome."

I loved having a best friend like her. "You have to say nice things, you're my best friend."

"You're not pretty all of the time. Some mornings you look like shit, so if you sleep with him, don't do it after you've had a lot to drink. Those are your break the mirror days."

"Thanks. I'll keep inebriation in mind. I wished you could have been there. Are you ever going to graduate, graduate school?" Seems like Sabrina had been attending classes forever and her education cut into our social time.

She chuckled. "At some point I guess. I have to work too. I have to come up with a thesis. I need a Sugar Daddy to keep me while I finish school. Maybe this Jordan has a friend."

"Bri, let me see where this goes before I start asking about a Sugar Daddy for you?"

Loud sigh. "Well, crap, if you insist. I love you, so I hope everything goes well."

"Love you, too. You'll be the first to know."

****

Jordan did call three days later. Three days of an agonizing wait. Sure, I could have called him. I'm an

15

adult woman with a career, but I wanted him to want me. When we talked, he asked to meet for lunch. I agreed a middle of the day date was a great idea. I had just an hour for lunch, and if lunch turned into a disaster, I could survive a short disaster. Then I could lament for years about the hot guy who wasn't so hot.

To my dread, things were far from horrible, and I had to leave to go back to work, but just before we left the deli, he asked if we could go to dinner on Friday evening. The sensible side of me wanted to play hard to get, but the too hot for him side, swung a bat at the sensible side, and we agreed to meet at *Ernie's Steak House* for dinner.

At least the sensible side wasn't quite ready to get into a car with him. She wanted to know him a little better first. Although, if the opportunity presented itself, I might be coaxed into bed with this god of my fantasy.

When I arrived at *Ernie's,* Jordan was waiting in the lobby, and I had to shut my eyes. You know there's moment when you think something just couldn't possibly get any better? Well there he stood revealing an even hotter version of what I considered perfection when we met at the fundraiser. Was a breeze ruffling his hair, or were my fantasies happening in real time?

He wore dark jeans, a white dress shirt, and a black leather jacket. I said a silent *Dayyammn.* Good thing he had no face stubble because a sandpaper scene would have been too much for me to bear. Even now, he appeared as if he just left a photo shoot for Men Who Make you Go Weak in the Knees, Indianapolis version.

My gaze aimed to his white shirt. "You like living dangerously, don't you?"

"If you only knew." He smiled and raised an

eyebrow. "There will be a table between us so I feel relatively safe…at least for now."

Why did his comment give me chills?

Stop it. But my command went unheeded by the butterflies rocketing around in my stomach. His semblance of cool unnerved me, and his air of confidence made me feel like a virgin on an offering pyre. Once we sat down and ordered drinks, I chose white wine this time, and my nerves calmed. He laughed with little effort, told stupid jokes, and was interested in what I had to say. He asked about my job and if I liked what I did. My job, not so much. Him definitely yes.

"So how long have you worked at Millennial Publishing?"

The server set two cups of *Ernie's* special bean soup in front of us. "Um, about three years. I taught high school English for two years before I went to work there."

"You were a teacher?" He spooned a mouthful of soup. "I bet all the kids wanted in your class. Cool, young, hot teacher. Why'd you quit?"

Hot. He just said I was hot.

"I didn't mind the kids. The parents, though, ugh." I shook my head at nightmarish reminder anyone is allowed to be a parent. "Parents drove me nuts. Either they didn't care or their only concern was how an A minus would affect their son or daughter's entry into the most prestigious universities in the country. Because of course their kid was the brightest one ever born on earth or any other planet with a modicum of life." I tore a piece of bread and dipped it into the soup. Not the thing to do in public, but too late now.

Jordan's gaze followed my hand dipping bread in the soup. *Shit. Bad choice.* He dipped his, and I released the breath I didn't realize I was holding.

"So what don't you like about your job now?"

"I guess maybe I'm bored. I don't know. I'm reading the same things over and over. They just have a different title. I need something new and different in my life."

"So find something new and different."

Mischief and mystery loomed behind those blue eyes. I shrugged. "I got bills to pay, and I admit starting something new is a little scary."

Jordan tore off another piece of bread and popped it into his mouth. "Sometimes, a little scary is what makes life interesting. Knowing what you're doing every day gets old. Every now and then, you need to push yourself to a limit you didn't know you had. Every challenge has its rewards."

He told me he was the marketing manager for a promotions company. He loved his job. In a city known for hosting hundreds of conventions annually, Indianapolis offered visitors a myriad of options, and Jordan said his company represented clients interested in making their events special.

"So why do you love your job?" I asked.

As our server neared our table, Jordan stopped him. "Could you bring us a bottle of Merlot?"

I cocked my head.

"I'm feeling a little adventurous tonight. Anyway, back to your question." He folded his hands together and rested his elbows on the table. "My job is different every day. I get to do many interesting things. I meet some incredibly fascinating...and challenging people, and I get to be in charge, making sure everyone is happy."

I could easily see Jordan in a position of leadership. With his smooth velvet voice, he could talk me into killing my grandmother. Good thing she died five years ago.

Between the bread, the Merlot, bean soup, and conversation, my belly and mind filled with the joy of having a non-disastrous first date at a first-rate restaurant.

When dinner arrived, my comfort level dropped exponentially. I didn't have food issues, but now a fifty-dollar New York strip graced my plate, and I faced a dilemma. If I ate all of steak plus the mashed potatoes and creamed spinach, then would he be like "wow, this chick eats. Can I afford her?" But then again, if I hardly ate any of my dinner, then he might think me wasteful and too worried about my weight—which at times was a constant issue for me, and most women I know.

In the end, my appetite made the decision to eat most of the meal, leaving a small amount of each selection on the plate, but declaring how wonderful the steak tasted. I detected no garlic in the meal, so I remained confident about what my breath would be like if he would be so inclined to kiss me. I sipped another glass of wine just to be sure, and by sip, I mean I nursed the thing. I didn't want this date to end.

After dinner, we strolled around Monument Circle, which was the exact center of Indianapolis, housing the Soldiers and Sailors Monument, a two hundred and eighty-four foot tall obelisk. Jordan spoke of how his company paid for several groups of children to visit the place during Christmas time. Thousands of lights hung from the top, creating what Indianapolis labeled the World's Tallest Christmas Tree. When he described the joy the children experienced, I tingled with the sensation of what it must be like to be a child during the holidays.

By the time we finished our walk, the butterflies had absorbed the wine, but a nauseous sense of melancholy crept into my body.

Our date neared the end.

"I want to walk you to your car." We stood face to face under the glow of a corner streetlight, oblivious to the pedestrians skirting around us to cross the street.

"I got lucky and scored street parking just a block down the street."

"I still would like to walk with you. Just to be safe."

The brief five minute-walk to my car at least extended our evening. Standing near my door, just far enough away not to impede oncoming traffic, we stood in an awkward silence. Was he going to kiss me or not?

I got my answer when his lips attached to mine in a gentle caressing, chaste and too short kiss. Still though, his lips ignited a fire, and I couldn't help but remember Danny Morgan. Danny from high school, who became the love of my life, my fantasy future husband, and the recipient of my virginity. We lasted three months, and until now, he was the best kisser in the world.

Danny had been dethroned, drawn, and quartered.

Jordan stepped away, his ice-blue gaze freezing me in place. I licked my lips to taste him when he demolished any personal space between us and descended upon my mouth. This time, not so gentle, but rather possessive. His tongue circled my lips as he palmed my cheeks with his hands, keeping my head immobile. I braced myself, placing my hands on the hood of my car.

I could not breathe.

With little coaxing, I opened my mouth letting him inside, tasting the rich oak and cherry of the wine on his tongue. He prodded to go deeper, and I fought the sensation my legs would give out. Catching my tongue with his teeth, he nibbled at first, and then tickled the roof of my mouth. I became aware of myself bending backward over the hood, but Jordan released my head to wrap his arms around my waist, holding me steady, warming my body in the January chill.

I opened my eyes when he broke our connection millimeter by millimeter. The ice blue in his was now a deep cobalt.

He brushed a stray hair from my cheek and whispered in my ear. "I don't want you to forget me."

My mouth kept opening, but no words had the gumption, or the ability to piece together a phrase.

"I hope we can continue what we've started. I quite like the taste of you."

I swallowed hard. "Me too," said the woman whose career was words. *Fucking brilliant.*

Holy shit, he was a master of mouth play. I was beginning to think I was dreaming this whole thing because what man is perfectly perfect? Somewhere, there had to be a flaw or something weird about Jordan Caldera.

Friday's dinner turned into brunch on Sunday—which turned into an afternoon of watching football at my apartment, which turned into ordering takeout for Sunday dinner, which led to a make out session I'd only witnessed in movies. One I assumed high schoolers still did, not someone who was about to turn thirty and a guy almost thirty-five.

After one weekend, we were a couple.

Jordan was different from other men I ever met—easy for him to love sports and shopping equally. He gave me a true sense of security when we were together. He opened doors for me, walked on the street side of me when we were out, and he made sure I stayed close when a crowd started to gather.

This guy got me. Understanding why a woman might be upset—what guy commands such a skill? And when was the last time a man even feigned interest in my moods? Yep, he possessed the intuition of a woman wrapped up in a delicious broad-shouldered body with a tight ass, velvet tongue, and an oceany scent with built in ability to induce my cootch to pucker.

Still, we hadn't had sex.

We had been dating several weeks with lots of soft caresses that more often than not led to a heavy-duty make out session, but we—or I should say 'he,' always stopped just short of the bedroom. Afterward, I stomped home and ripped my vibrator from the drawer. I had to go to a warehouse store to buy batteries, because the eight-packs weren't even close to enough.

One evening, when he had upped my frustration level to nuclear, I asked him why he didn't want to have sex with me, and he said, "Angel, and you are my Angel, I want our trip to heaven to be very special. So when the time is right, and I make love to you, you *will* remember."

Gulp.

I cried. No man I ever knew had said such things to

me.

He kissed my tears away from my cheeks. I cried harder. He gave up and retrieved a box of tissues.

Two weeks later, Jordan asked me to come to his condo after work, and he would make dinner. I had been to his place on the canal a few times. The view from the top floor was worth the lofty price. Standing on the balcony, one could see quite a lot of the canal snaking its way through parts of the city. People jogging and walking their dogs frequented the cement sidewalks on both sides of the water. Gondolas, paddleboats, and ducks cruised the water in the summer months. The whole package was picturesque, peaceful, and much better than my one bedroom apartment toward the south end of town, although my neighborhood was going through a renaissance of sorts, attracting up and comings, artists, cafes and boutiques.

Since Jordan often worked longer in the day at his job, than I did at mine, I shopped the downtown mall to see if I could find anything better to wear than I currently wore. For half a week's salary, I found many things I liked, but purchased none, deciding paying off my school loans trumped almost every considered purchase. He often said I had a sense for fashion. I had a sense for fashion at a reduced price.

At seven, I knocked on his door. When door flew open, Jordan grabbed me by the waist, hauling me inside and up against the wall. I gasped, and before I could say anything, he trapped my wrists high above me, while his mouth settled firmly on my lips. "Open," he commanded as he shoved his tongue inside, sweeping circles around my tongue.

Beer. He drank a beer sometime before I arrived.

The hint of yeasty sweet apple on his tongue reminded me of an autumn day.

Once the shock wore off, I returned his passion teasing him by keeping my tongue out of range before attacking again. Much to my dismay, he eased away ending the assault.

I smiled still reeling from his welcome. "I hope I'm not in the wrong apartment because the guy who lives here is a phenomenal kisser."

"You think so?" He nibbled my neck sending a tingling all the way to my toes. Damn, I could do this all day.

"Yep." He had already changed out of suit and into faded blue jeans and a well-worn Duke T-shirt. The scent of fresh garlic wafted through the air. "Smells awesome, what we having?"

"Margherita pizza and tomato salad."

"So now I understand the kiss. After so much garlic, kissing might be put on hold for the night."

He cupped my face with his hands. "Wrong. I don't care what you've eaten. I want to taste everything you've got."

After dinner, he produced brownies with caramel icing. Seeing my excitement at such sweet decadence he said, "Don't get too excited, I bought these, but I got them at Taylors so they should be good."

Inhaled best described my action. "I don't care," I muffled through a full mouth. "Brownies are the most perfect food on earth." He might as well know the unabridged woman I was.

"Then maybe I will try to make them sometime." He smiled as he munched a bite not as gigantic as the one I stuffed into my mouth.

After dessert, we walked outside to the balcony. The mid-winter temps didn't set the best scene for casual relaxing, but he wrapped his arms around my waist and kissed my neck. I'd always loved warm weather, but this tropical trip in the middle of winter traveled all of the way down to my toes. Any more, and I'd break out in a sweat.

We cuddled and stared at the clear dark sky, but brilliant with hundreds of stars twinkling and casting a light to the fog our breaths created.

"Wait here, I'll be right back," he whispered. I shivered with cold when he left, but just minutes later, Jordan was back.

"Come with me." He grabbed my hand tugging me away from the balcony. Our destination, as I suspected, his bedroom. When I stepped into his room, I discovered why he left me alone to freeze. In his absence from the balcony, Jordan had arranged several vanilla-scented candles around the darkened room. The golden glow generated dancing shadows along the wall, illuminating the king bed with a wrinkle-free gray-and-white-striped comforter. The mahogany frame sported four tall posts with rod iron cross beams connecting the posts at both the headboard and footboard. More rod iron rails decorated the curved wood of the headboard.

This was a man's room.

He faced me, rubbing my arms with his hands. "Will you stay the night with me?" he asked. His ice-blue eyes now dark and intense.

The huge lump in my throat wouldn't budge "Yes," I squeaked.

His laugh rang like music through the air. He raised his hand to my chin. "You are my Angel,

Emma."

Wanting to cut the time of getting into the bed, I assisted in removing my sweater. I take that back. I pretty much ripped the thing over my head. I did put forethought into the evening and had worn my black lacy bra and matching underwear.

Somewhere during his orgasmic assault on my neck, collarbone and lips, my slacks, heels, and hosiery also disappeared. How he accomplished such a feat, I still am not sure.

I reclaimed enough of my senses to rip his shirt out of his waistband and over his head, revealing his body for the first time. And what I beheld was heart stopping—his olive-skinned, protruding pecs, rounded biceps, V-shaped god of a man body. "Oh my God," I was sure I said in my head, but from Jordan's lofty, but amused eyebrows, I said the words aloud.

He smiled making me more embarrassed than I already was. "You like what you see?"

"I do." I drew circles around his nipples with my fingertips. His sharp intake of breath encouraged my exploration. His coarse chest hairs tickled my palms with the motion of my hands.

"I like everything I see and what I don't see."

His hands skimmed the tops of my breasts before making a slow calculated descent to caress my nipples still tucked in my bra. For someone who hated her breasts fondled, my whole body shuddered as he unclasped my bra before taking the nipple to his mouth, sucking and licking. My previous boyfriends didn't attend the same boob arousal university as Jordan. Dear God, I wasn't sure how much longer I could hold out, and we had not even gotten to the good part.

"Breathe, Angel. Breathe."

When was the last time someone had to tell me to breathe?

The process of undoing his jeans shifted my concentration away from the vigorous aspirating of my chest, but as soon as I unzipped the denim, and yanked down his boxer briefs, the beast sprang forward, landing just above my belly button. *Oh, shit.* Again, I was wrong the words being in my head.

He stopped and lifted his attention to me. He smiled, cocking one eyebrow high, and finished undressing, kicking his clothes away from us. Jordan leaned his head to the hollow of my neck. Like a furnace blazing against my skin, his tongue blistered me with each swipe. I grabbed his stone biceps as he walked me backward toward the mattress. My nerves had lost all patience.

"I think we need to be in the bed," he said in a husky tone.

Finally.

When the back of my knees touched the bed, I collapsed never taking my eyes from Jordan's naked body framed in the golden glow of the candles, and again I forgot to breathe.

This image, this phenomenon invading my senses had me giddy with arousal and committing this canvas of perfection to my memory forever. Better than any dream. Better than any movie I'd watched or any book I'd ever read. I believed without a doubt, this man would so touch me to a depth, his prints would remain on my soul forever.

Jordan reached for the packet in the drawer next to the bed, tearing open the condom. We paused as he rolled the protection down his erection.

"Lay back, Angel." He didn't bother to draw the comforter down, so I slid to the center of the mattress as Jordan climbed in next to me.

What I expected, and what I received were singular. I anticipated a profound intensely thorough and immediate fucking. Instead of blessing me with the fantasy I created in my head, his cock rested against the tender skin of my inner thigh, as if waiting for the green light to dive in. His mouth, on the other hand, found my belly. His tongue trailed down my stomach, my hip, the inside of my thigh, and all while his erection rubbed my skin with a weird sensation of fire and need.

Electrified, the hairs on my arms almost hurt from awkward standing. I couldn't control the need to kiss him so I snatched his hair to guide him back to me. His blue gaze pierced through me like a spear.

"I wasn't finished," he said with a mixture of displeasure and lust.

"I need you up here," I told him.

He kissed my neck, biting tiny nips, carving a path to my mouth, forcing his tongue harder and deeper than ever before. His silken strands of hair slipped through my fingers.

Jordan unclasped my hands from his hair and held both over my head with one hand. With the other, he inserted a finger inside, touching me deep, and my responsive body clenched. I wiggled my hands away from his grip and grabbed his hair again as I let out a moan. In one swift effort, he captured my hands back over my head. "Leave them," and I recognized from his firm tone, I would do as he said.

"Just let me touch you. Let yourself feel. Plenty of

time for me," he said.

"Jordan, if you don't take care of business here real soon, I'm gonna die."

A snicker deep in his throat didn't help. "You need to learn some patience," he whispered, but added, "Maybe I'm a little anxious, too."

He withdrew his finger.

"Okay, then, wish granted," he said plunging deep into me.

The sudden stretching disabled my breathing, and my body tensed with something between "Oh shit," and "Hell yes."

"Are you all right? Open your eyes, Angel."

"I'm fine. I just wasn't expecting you to be so…well…large." I swallowed. "But big's a good thing. It's just…an adjustment."

"I can't change the size of my dick."

I touched his cheek. His face registered honest concern for my welfare regarding his grandiose cock. "Really, it's fine, more than fine."

He kissed my forehead and captured my wayward hand again. "Let me touch you."

My chest heaved with another intake of oxygen I know I would hold.

Jordan wielded his weapon inside of me with rhythm, shoving, retreating, and with every frenzied pump, I escaped and freed myself from every moment of disappointing sex I'd ever had. This was so worth all of the two-minute Toms, bad hygiene, and whiskey dick encounters I'd experienced since the first time a cock gained entrance, and nobody ever was able to fill me like this. Fill me so much, I thought he'd poked a hole into my stomach. What he really did was fill me clear into my soul.

Then he pulled out.

What the fuck?

My angst was short-lived. He inserted his finger again, rubbing my clit, and I teetered on the edge of a cavern of bliss. No way in hell was I going to stop this dive into the orgasm cosmos.

He released my hands and removed his finger to trap my waist in his embrace. Jordan plunged hard again, deeper than before. I never conceived the idea my grotto was so vast. Like an explorer in a new land, Jordan cut a path to my soul.

"Remember," he whispered. "Hands off."

I grabbed the pillow beneath my head and wanted to rip the stuffing from the case. With the "no touch" edict in effect, keeping quiet would not happen, and my single concern was I hoped the walls were thick because… "Oh shit, Oh shit, I… Oh my…"

Somehow, despite my own moans, my ears picked up Jordan's glorious revelation, "Fuck, Fuck. Here it goes." We were in complete synchronicity.

He collapsed on my chest. His heartbeat drowning out the sound of my own pounding.

"Can I touch you, now?" I teased.

"I'm all sweaty, Angel."

I brushed back a silky handful of hair now stuck on his forehead and discovered a light sheen of sweat. "Maybe, sweat's a turn on for me." *Starting today.*

I caressed his perspiration covered back, reveling in my glory and sense of peace with this incredible man, who called me Angel. How did I get so lucky?

I licked my salty fingers. "You taste good."

He brushed the wet strands of hair from the

forehead, touching his own to mine. "Maybe, you'd like to taste another part of me."

"I'm on it." I attempted to shove from beneath him.

"Not now. Another time."

Another time. Yes. This was the beginning of my education in fine art of good sex.

There was a change in our relationship in one night in more ways than just sex. The sex was constant, wild, and fulfilling, but Jordan became part of me. He wanted to know everything about me. He touched me at every opportunity, and the physical sense accounted for the smallest percentage. Jordan's strength and confidence guided me.

With him, I was different.

I discovered a woman who both excited and scared me.

Emma was now Angel, and Angel was rising.

"I love you, Angel. I've known from our first date I would love you."

He was perfect.

Chapter Three

So many thoughts and memories swirled in my head as I allowed Jessica to catch up typing her notes on the laptop. As soon as I'd started talking, my nerves lessened with every sentence.

This is who I am now.

I'm not ashamed, but my lifestyle isn't accepted out in the open, especially now with all of the "empower women," campaigns, but these choices give me power. I feel if I talk, people might not understand our choices are different, but being on the fringe doesn't mean they are wrong.

Jessica stopped writing. "From what you've said, your husband seems rather normal. How long were you together before he asked you to go BDSM?"

I laughed and twirled a fake strand of hair. "Normal is a very subjective term. But in answer to your question, he didn't mention anything. He didn't say anything until he asked me to marry him."

Jessica's eyes widened. "I bet that was a little bit of a shock."

"Understatement," I said.

"So you had no clue. Was there anything you noticed and should have tipped you off?"

I pondered her question for a few seconds. "Well I guess in retrospect, there were some subtle hints. Subtlety is not my strong suit. I never picked up on them."

"Like what?"

"The first night I stayed over, he provided a toothbrush for me and had clothes for me to wear the next day." I thought more about the signs I completely missed.

"Ummm. We would be out shopping, and he would pick out things, you know, high neck blouses, turtlenecks, scarves and ask if I liked them. At the time, I believed he considered them classic and timeless style. The initial investment was higher, but the cost over time was much lower. My manner of dress displayed business casual, while his projected success. I mean in his job, it's important for everyone to be well put together. My job, not as much."

Jessica asked. "So what does your husband do? Why does he require a certain image?"

I caught her attempt to dig into our identities. "He worked, and I believe one of my ground rules. No questions regarding our identities."

Busted.

"I'm sorry. I didn't intend to come off that way," she said.

Sure.

Back to what I was talking about. "When we were out where there were lots of people, he would be…"

"Possessive?" she interrupted.

"No, more like protective, especially when there were a lot of men in the group."

"Had he been cheated on in his past relationships?" Jessica asked.

"I think so, but it was more that he made sure everyone knew we were a couple."

Jessica's fingertips pounded the keyboard. "Isn't that kind of the same thing?"

"No. He's never told me not to do something or not to talk to someone. Well, there was one."

"There were other things, too," I said. "In the bedroom, he really wanted to guide the direction of our lovemaking, I guess you would say."

"And you were okay with…leadership?"

"I liked that part of him."

****

Jordan wanted me to stay the weekend again. Just like other weekends, he told me to bring myself as is, and he would have everything I needed waiting for me. I was beginning to accumulate a nice wardrobe at his condo. He had very good taste, at least in winter clothes. From the cashmere turtlenecks, to silk scarves he elegantly wrapped around my neck, a part of me wondered if he worked in the fashion industry. Cotton, silk, cashmere, wool. The fabrics were always natural.

While the bears loved the February chill at the zoo, the cold was a little brisk for me, and became more of an opportunity for Jordan to wrap himself around me. "I don't usually like the cold, but I'm kinda liking this." I liked the hot body warming me as we watched the polar bear splashing around in his artic pool.

"Just wait until we get home," he whispered in my ear. *Home*. I liked the sound of *home*.

A few hours later, with a blanket wrapped around me, I relaxed on the sofa watching the flames from the fireplace dance and swirl. Jordan called from the kitchen. "Hot chocolate or wine?"

"What is your intent? To warm me up or get me drunk?"

He stepped into view. "If getting you drunk was my intent, then the wine would serve both purposes. Do I have to get you drunk to sleep with me?"

"Sleeping, huh?" I raised a curious eyebrow.

"At some point," he teased back. He flew to me like Spiderman, ripped the blanket away, picked me up and slung me over his back in a firefighter's carry. "Time's up. You didn't choose, so I did."

"So which one am I getting?"

"You're getting me."

"I can live with that."

He dropped me in the middle of the bed then said, "Arms up."

I raised my arms as he slipped the sweater over my head, leaving a lacy camisole and the white lace bra he had purchased for me. "Those too," he pointed and began pulling the camisole over my head as well. I unhooked the bra myself, but Jordan slipped the straps from my shoulders from me, kissing my bareness as he finished my undressing.

I shivered when his magic tongue thrusted against mine, asking—no demanding I give him more. He slung me onto the bed, and I started to undo my jeans, but he stopped me. "Not yet, Angel."

He yanked his Purdue sweatshirt over his head, tossing the garment to the floor as if on fire before he scrambled on top of me. My gazed darted around like a cat watching a laser pointer—I couldn't keep track of where his hands landed. His middle finger on his right hand had a small callous, and when he started caressing my cheeks, the uneven skin snagged across my skin as his hand slithered to the hollow of my throat.

"Open your eyes, Angel. Look at me."

I had no idea my eyes were closed. My reward for opening them—the icy blue of his, both sincere and sensual in the dim light of the room.

He tasted like Christmas, and his tongue hypnotized my mouth—commanding my lips to accept and also give. Who knew under your arms was an erogenous zone? At least for me, flicks of his tongue and nips of his teeth released a squeal of pain, which transformed into a moan of need.

Oh, you bastard. I now got his cruel motive by not letting me take off my jeans. The ache in my clit grew to an exponential level, and I could do nothing to relieve the torture. His hands were elsewhere, and my access was blocked.

"Jordan?" I managed to whisper when he underwent a brief respite from kisses.

"I have a real problem, here." I gasped with ragged breaths.

I wiggled my hips, and his curious stare told me he was aware of what my problem was, but he played along. "And what would that be?"

"Something down there needs attention," I said.

God, his smile just killed me.

"Really?" he said with a raised eyebrow. "I think I'll make you wait a little longer. You need to learn a little patience."

"Why is this always about me? What about you? Don't you want anything out of this?" I think I was whining. I've never been a whiner, but this situation called for whining.

His blue eyes grew intense. "I want everything out of this. The difference is I can control myself, something you need to learn, and when you do, your release is even more powerful."

"Do I have to start learning now?" I trembled and wiggled some more.

"You need to learn something every day," he said before going back to punishing me by tracing his tongue along the contours of my neck.

When he unbuttoned my jeans, I swear my vagina said "Thank God." He dragged them down just enough to insert two fingers inside of me. I jumped from the sheer shock of impending gratification.

"Easy, Angel, he cautioned. "Relax."

How in Hell could I relax when a lightning bolt of foreplay had entered my pussy?

Three deep breaths later, I had recovered enough to enjoy the feeling of his massaging without feeling I was going to climax.

Jordan completed my undressing but left on his jeans. By the manifestation of the bulge at his zipper, the beast behind the metal wanted to pry open the bars of its cage.

I was sure he would unzip and join me, but I was so wrong. When he removed his fingers, grabbed my hips, and inserted his tongue, my body convulsed with electrocution. *Damn*. I looked down because I was convinced I'd plastered myself to the ceiling. "Oh damn, Jordan, Shit."

"Easy, sweetie. Soon, very soon." That transcendental mouth was making me want to go all Walden Pond, because his tongue inside of me was the most natural and spiritual thing I'd ever experienced. So, I lifted just enough to yank the pillow from under my head to smash over my face. Jordan laughed at my struggles, but he kept tongue rolling, swishing, and caressing my core. Add to this scenario, the unusual fact he had not shaved, the stubble rubbing me was pure heaven and hell in alternating swipes.

"Are you ready, Angel?" he asked.

Still with a pillow over my head, I screamed, "Fuck me, yes, dammit."

"Such language. Okay. Let it go, Baby, let it go."

Waves and waves of uncontrollable spasms washed over me, my hips bucking and me screaming into the pillow, until I was silent and damp from exhaustion.

Jordan threw the pillow on the floor as he inched closer to my face. "Are you still breathing?"

"Barely."

"That's a plus." Jordan hopped up from the bed, dropped his jeans and grabbed a condom out of the nightstand drawer. As he began unrolling, I said. "You know, I'm on birth control."

"I know," he said sitting on the bed. He leaned over to kiss me, and I tasted myself on his tongue. "Nothing wrong with being safe."

He crawled on top of me with the prowess of a stalking lion—his penis pausing as if waiting for a signal during our kisses. I have to admit, it's a little weird to be kissing and what you taste is you, but despite the taste test, I was consumed with him more and more as he filled my body with his—his hard and smooth erection against my eager wet walls. Slow, measured, and luxurious, Jordan presided over the pace. I still believed even though he was inside me now, these strokes were mine, too. I could feel him getting close, but he stopped.

"You're beautiful, Angel. I love you."

I needed him cemented to me so I made a vise with

my arms as his thrusts became faster and faster until he roared with the sound of his own release echoing off the walls.

We both fell into a deep slumber. I attached myself to his side with my head on his chest. I don't know how much time passed, but from a faraway fog in my brain, Jordan called my name. My eyes were heavy but trying to wake up. His hand on my cheek did the trick.

Crusty residue broke away as I cracked open my eyes. "You've exhausted me."

His eyes darkened, while easy smile turned serious, and the hairs on my arms stood up. "Here," he said. "I need you to sit up."

I positioned myself up against the headboard. "No, here," he said as he hauled me to his lap.

"Emma, I need to talk with you about something."

Emma. He never called me Emma anymore. Always Angel. Now I was scared, feeling a sick feeling deep in my stomach. "Oh?"

He brushed a stray hair from my face. "Don't look so sad," he said.

As much as I loved staring in the icy blueness of his eyes, now I couldn't. Anytime a conversation starts with *we need to talk*, things never go well for the person on the other end.

"It's serious, Emma, but I hope it'll be good."

Okay. My spirits lifted a little, but I was still concerned.

He touched my chin. "Please, I just ask you to hear everything I have to say before you say anything."

"OooOkaaay."

"Emma."

Damn, he was using my name again.

"I think you are the sweetest and most beautiful woman I've ever known. I love you. I have never entertained such love for anyone. I feel like you are for me, only me. I would love to be married to you."

My heart jumped.

"But there is something about me…there is a need I have you might find horrible or unacceptable.

My heart sank.

I shook from the inside, or so I believed. Jordan covered my shoulders with the sheet.

"Maybe this conversation shouldn't be done naked. I just feel I should talk to you now," he said.

Whereas before, I couldn't breathe from ecstasy, now my chest tightened and my stomach reeled from the impending doom I anticipated.

"Emma. I have this need my wife always know I'm always there. That you are mine."

"I…" I started to say I would be always his, but he put his finger to my lips.

"Please Angel, let me finish.

"My tattoo. Have you ever wondered what it represents?"

My hand slid to the ink above his breast. "Sometimes, but then I get sidetracked with what we're doing and forget to ask you."

He swallowed hard. "This tattoo symbolizes a life I used to live then walked away from. I didn't want to go back, until I met you."

"I don't understand." Each word he said confused and unnerved me. What was this symbol, and why did our relationship trigger a memory?

His finger grazed the black symbol inked into his skin. "In some ways, I wish I had never gotten this. I've had the ink awhile and at the time the symbol meant something to me, and then it didn't, and now you do."

"Jordan, God dammit! Stop. Just tell me." Instead of soothing me, his rhythmic massaging of my shoulders freaked me out. I could feel a tentativeness transferring from his hands to my own nerves. Whatever he was trying to tell me was going to change our relationship.

"This triskelion can symbolize many things to many people, but for me and a large number of people, this a BDSM reference."

"Okay," Where was he going with this? "Are you saying you were involved, then you weren't and now…"

"Do you know what BDSM is?" He stopped massaging and those ice blues froze me in place.

"Of course I know what it is! I do, but I guess not in detail." I had no clue what he meant. I was somewhere between not wanting to be stupid and naïve and not wanting him to think I liked to hang from the ceiling…if suspension was what he meant. BDSM was never on my radar. Maybe I was a little curious. The only other place I'd had sex besides a bed was in a hayloft when I was in college. Yep, literally a roll in the hay.

His ice-cold hands raised mine to his lips. He kissed my knuckles, and the contrast of heat against the cold was indicative of the conversation I was afraid we might have. I wanted to lighten this heavy blanket of anxiety draped around us. "Well, you're not putting a finger anywhere up my body because it's like a damn iceberg."

He laughed, kissing my fingers before his

expression turned serious again. "When I was in college, I found this sexual world answered a lot questions I had about myself. I was pretty sexually active during college."

Of course you were. Just look at you. Who would turn you down?

"But the sex just wasn't enough. Something was missing for me until I found a group…A group who practiced BDSM, and I realized what I was missing. I needed something different in the bedroom. Answered a lot of questions for me. Before, I thought I was crazy, but I'm just different."

"But Jordan, what we do isn't…" He put his fingers to my lips stopping my words.

"Emma, let me finish."

His agitation with my interrupting was growing. "I'm sorry. I'm a little out of sorts here."

He cupped my cheek, his fingers now warming to my face. "I'm the one who's sorry. I'm not doing a very good job of explaining what I'm trying to say."

He captured my hands again in his, but now, they were gentle and warm. "I was in this group for a very long time. There's way more people who are into the life than you think. A few years ago, though, I walked away from the group, the life, everything."

I know he was waiting for me to say something, but I waited, trying to exercise some of the patience he said I didn't have.

"Some things happened that bothered me and made me question maybe the life wasn't right for me, but then I met you." He rested his forehead against mine. "I met you and all of those feelings flooded back. The things I want to do to you. The things I want you to do for me. I can't see straight I love you so much, but I want you to be mine. I want everything about your body, soul, and mind to belong to me."

Right then I wanted to crawl inside of him forever.

"If you become my wife, I want to re-enter the life, and I want you to wear a collar for me."

Wait. What?

Maybe I was losing my hearing. "What?"

"I know you heard me, Emma. I would want you to wear a collar."

He paused just long enough I seized my turn to talk. "I know what you said, but I am not sure I understand. All of the time? For how long? Why, is my biggest question? This is very bizarre to me. Do you not trust me? Have you been cheated on or something?" I was rambling, but if there was ever a time for rambling this was the time. Someone grabbed a hammer and shattered the glass house surrounding my life.

He glanced toward the window before slipping the sheet from my shoulders and tightening his arms around me. "Yes, I understand this disclosure is all very strange to you. Not for me though. I've been this way a very long time. Yes, I've been cheated on, but cheating has nothing to do with you, or why I'm asking you this. Though I'm sure not forever, still I'd want you to. For me, collaring represents our relationship is complete, and you're not just married to me, but part of me, always."

Again, we touched foreheads. I closed my eyes, listening to the silence in the room. The sheet fell away, but Jordan's arms encircled my bare shoulders and every unnerving word he said to me in the last few minutes disappeared into the clean ocean scent of this man I loved so much. His body radiated with strength and passion attempting to calm my frazzled mind.

Still in our embrace, he said. "Collaring can elicit a very erotic feeling, a feeling of extreme love and devotion. Emma, this just didn't come to me. All of this time with you, I've been learning and understanding what kind of woman you are. You're a submissive. You're who I've been wanting my whole life."

My turn arrived to stare at whatever wasn't happening outside of the window. I was hearing his words, but this whole confession emerged like such a weird dream. Had our sex been so out of body I was hallucinating? A tender and warm hand gripped my chin, forcing me to look at him.

I had to ask. "If I say 'no' to this, what happens to us?"

Always so expressive, his eyes churned with blue anguish. "I don't know. I'm not going to give you up, but it'll be hard knowing what you are and not being able act on it."

Short and to the point.

My body trembled, and I couldn't control the shakes. For all of the times I always had something to say, my brain refused my request to form a word, but one fact slapped me upside the head. Here's the glitch, the rub, the footnote. My Mr. Perfect. My flawless lover had a secret.

"Emma. I don't need you to answer me now, or tomorrow, or even next week. I want you to think about all of this and make the right decision for you."

He hugged me tighter into his arms, and I rested my head on his chest. I am not sure whose heart was beating the loudest, but they were in unison. I just lay there for I don't even know how long. At some point, I collapsed into exhausted slumber, because the next thing I remember was Jordan's fingertips circling my naked shoulders, urging me to wake up. The sun was streaming though the bedroom window.

"Angel," he whispered. "What do you want for breakfast?"

I opened my eyes to see those blue eyes and mussed up hair in my face. That was some crazy dream I had last night. I would keep the details to myself. "Good morning. I really slept hard last night."

He smiled and raked his forefinger across my cheek. "You fell asleep in my lap. I just let you sleep naked. Worked for me, though."

Lap…naked… Nope, no dream. He did ask me to marry him, and there was a big 'But' attached.

Chapter Four

"I wonder how many women have ever had that question asked of them?" Jessica said as she typed.

I sucked a long drink of water from the bottle. "I am sure it's not the weirdest thing men have asked women, but BDSM came out of left field."

"Obviously you said yes, but how long did you take before you decided, and how did you decide? When you make out a 'pro and con' list, the very idea had to have been weird. Did you tell anyone? What about your best friend. What did she say?" Jessica stopped typing. Fellow rambler.

She was fascinated I could tell. "For a couple of weeks, I worked on research, but failed to find any useful or definitive answers. I didn't tell anyone. In fact, one friend of mine knows, and the discovery was purely an accident. When Sabrina found out, our friendship ended."

****

Jordan had not mentioned the subject of collaring again except to say I needed to think about what he was asking, so I deemed he was being honest when he told me to take my time with my decision.

We continued to date, had dinner, spent the night at each other's apartments, and did all of the things dating couples do. Even though, we had not spoken of our conversation again, I admit, our togetherness was not as easy as before. The huge elephant in the room would not budge.

Two weeks passed, and I asked Jordan to come over Friday to watch movies. I was not finding all of the answers I needed online so I had to be straight up with him and ask all of my questions.

I sat on one end of the sofa with my feet in his lap, while two *Transformers* movies played back to back. When the credits rolled on the last movie, I took the empty popcorn bowls to the kitchen. When I returned, I sucked a deep breath and sat down in his lap. "I have some questions," I said straight up.

He smoothed my hair away from my face. "I would be worried if you didn't," he said.

Just come right out and ask. "Are you a Dominant?"

His eyes widened. "Been online?"

"Maybe. Are you?"

He ran his hand through his hair, but a lock flopped back over his forehead distracting me. I loved his hair. "There is a multi-faceted answer, but as a yes or no question, I guess I would have to say yes."

"So you want me to be your submissive?" My research into collaring had led me to several BDSM web sites. I found information on Dominants and submissives, but not much on what he had asked me.

"Again a multi-faceted answer, but I will start with the first one."

The playful Jordan had left. Now his features were dark and serious. "Like I told you before, I was into the BDSM life. So much of the life suited me. Playing with people I didn't have to have a serious relationship with was attractive. Sometimes, though, you want a relationship, and they don't. Some subs had needs I just didn't want to fill. That being said, during the agreed upon period, the sub belonged to me. She was mine for those hours. Some are into extreme pain. I found I just couldn't administer to them. You have to be a responsible person though. You never want anyone to be hurt or permanently harmed."

The growing lump in my throat burned. "Why did you stop?"

"I stopped because I was no longer getting what I wanted or needed, but now, I feel I want to go back."

"Have you ever been engaged?"

"Yes."

"May I ask why the relationship ended? Was it because she wouldn't...you know?"

"You never just ask one question, do you?" but he wasn't irritated when he spoke.

"Nature of my work, I suppose."

"The engagement ended because she was more a Dominant in sexual nature, and in the bedroom, wasn't going to work for me. Although, she ended the relationship, not me after I caught her with someone else."

"So you think I'm submissive in nature?"

"Yes."

I frowned, not sure I liked where this was going."

"Not in all aspects, Emma, but during sex, you like it, when I guide you. You like it when I make you wait. Your climaxes are so much stronger. When you like something, Emma, you submit without a second thought."

"Is that the specific reason you think I'm submissive in nature?"

He touched my cheek. "Angel. I've been trying things out on you since we went out. I was so excited about you. Wrong of me, I'm sure. Every time I told you not to bring anything with you when you stayed with me, you didn't. You accepted what I had here for you. I've made decisions for you about several different things, and you accepted. And I also knew when the decision wasn't right for you."

"How did you know?"

"Because you would say so. When I said I was going to cook fish for dinner, you said you didn't like fish. When I picked out a certain movie, you would say you didn't want to see it. A lot of little things added up, and showed me how you are?"

"Me letting you pick out clothes, keeping my hands at bay and told when to climax told you I was submissive?"

He nodded with such conviction, I had little argument to support anything else.

"Other relationships you had. Why did they end?"

"Well, because I got tired of them never making a decision about anything." Oh, crap. He was right. Jordan made decisions, and I loved that about him without even realizing it. "Okay. I kind of understand now what you are saying about me, but why does a collar make the difference to you?"

"Emma. It binds you to me, a constant reminder I'm part of you, and I'm responsible for you and your well-being. That I love you and am for you and you alone. It's erotic. When you feel the collar around your neck, you think of us, and what we do together. For me, I don't feel I'm degrading you. It's symbolizing you're special and the single woman in my life. You are the powerful one, because you are giving me permission."

While he was talking, his fingers browsed my cheeks, my shoulders and brushed my hair away from my face. He wasn't trying to get me turned on, but he was. Maybe my arousal grew from his touch, or maybe just his words, but I still had more questions. "How much would I have to wear it? How long. I mean, like years or what?"

"You ask all of the right questions. Questions are a good thing. I would want you to wear it most of the time. I want to show you how exciting and fulfilling BDSM can be. I want to watch you bound, wet, and begging for release. Then I want to give you all of things and more. I want to fill you like no one ever has or ever will.

"That scares me a little, Jordan." Even though I admitted my fear, I couldn't help my arousal growing as he described what he wanted to do.

"I understand, but know this. I will never harm you, maybe make you uncomfortable, but I won't hurt you. Also, there are times when wearing one type of collar won't be convenient, so we'll have to change things up."

"But I can't go out in public wearing...you know."

"Most of the clothes I've bought for you, what are they?"

I recalled our shopping trips. Wow, he was checking me out, and I didn't even know. "Turtlenecks and scarves."

"It's easy to cover."

"But what about summer?"

"Not difficult. Scarves will work. By then you would adjust. You wouldn't even notice. It's not a large one, not even an inch wide."

He already had everything planned. "Someone might notice if I drop from heat stroke."

He laughed like that was the dumbest thing he'd ever heard and then kissed me. "You will not die of heat stroke. You aren't alone in this, and I've never seen bondage heats stroke headline in the news."

"I have one other question for you." I asked, and this one was very important to me.

"Okay, Emma, I'll always answer your questions honestly."

"Do you want children?"

My heart melted from the tenderness in his eyes and the most genuine smile I'd received from him. "Yes, Angel. I want children with you. I want as many children with you as we can have. I struggled with giving up the lifestyle. I don't want to let go. It's part of who I am, but I get so excited when I think about you joining me. I want this to be us not just me."

"Why didn't you just tell me in the first place?" I wondered.

"When I met you at the gala, I fell so hard for you. I couldn't wait to take you out. I didn't want to scare you off. I thought I could win you over with my charm and skills in the bedroom"—his eyes twinkled with the last remark—"before I dropped a bomb. Most people see BDSM as very abnormal, but for me, and a lot of others, our normal is a little different."

"Well, you didn't take long to win me over."

I had to get serious again. This was a life-changing decision I could only share with Jordan. I couldn't tell my family, friends, or co-workers. I barely understood what he was telling me. How could I expect anyone to understand why I was considering this life with him? "Thank you for talking with me. I still have a lot to think about."

"I know you do, and I won't pressure you." He embraced my face with gentle hands, kissing me with all of the love he proclaimed. I could feel he was getting an erection, but he ended the kiss. "I should go home," he said.

"Jordan?" I said as he was leaving.

"Yes?"

"Could I try before deciding?"

He turned back to me. "No, Emma. It's either all or nothing. That moment should be special to us. I'll show you some bondage toys if you want to try them."

I nodded yes, but the terrified lump in my throat refused to allow any words out of my mouth.

After he left my apartment, I climbed into bed thinking about our conversation. I was scared, but still shivered with the possibilities the whole idea stirred in me. While I had had many sexual experiences, none was as exhilarating as they were with Jordan. He was right. I did love when Jordan called all of the shots. When he told me not to touch him and to hold my climax, I'd bet my life I would die from the pure pleasure and pain I experienced.

I made a research decision.

The next day I drove out of the city to a pet store where I wouldn't run into anyone I knew. Standing in the aisle staring at the myriad of collars and leashes. I ran the gamut of emotion from a little naughty, kinky, excited, to frankly a little embarrassed. What was I doing? Jordan had told me no, and here I was trying to decide which dog collar I was going to take home and,

and I carried a secret I would never tell him. How could I question his honesty when I was here doing this behind his back?

I found a simple black leather collar about an inch and a half wide. I was within a few steps of the cash register when an alarm bell rang in my head. If I just bought the collar, then someone might think I was buying it for me. I mean, who buys a collar and nothing else. What a dumbass. Convinced everyone in the store was watching me, hyperventilation almost consumed me as much as it did the first time I bought alcohol before my twenty-first birthday. I calmed down enough to pick out a red leash and to grab a bag of dog biscuits on my way to the check out.

"Did you just get a new puppy?" the cashier asked as she rang them up.

"Yes," I gave the short answer.

"Well, the collar you picked out might be a little big for a puppy."

Oh, shit. Think of something. "She's a shelter dog, full grown. So this will be perfect."

"Oh great. That's wonderful you're rescuing. I have three rescue dogs, and they are so great. You want to see a picture?"

"No. I, uh," *Oh crap.* She pulled out a photo from her cashier's vest. Who does that? However, I had to admit the dogs were adorable.

"Thank you," I said as I handed her the money, and when she handed me my change, I bolted for the door.

I ripped the leash and biscuits from the bag, dropping them into the back of a pick-up truck parked next to my car. "Late Merry Christmas," I said.

Back at my apartment, I threw the bag deep into

the trash, just in case Jordan would be over and somehow find out about my experiment. Rummaging through my trash looking for contraband was not something Jordan would do, but by now, I swore he was hiding around every corner in my apartment.

Holding the collar in my hand, I fingered the leather, soft to touch, but still a bit rigid. I raised the strap to my nose to smell the scent of the new material. Would this be what I smelled? I stopped finding reasons to stall and put up my hair with a clip then wrapped the collar around my neck. I supported my possible future without fastening the buckle. I fucking shivered. Was this fear or anticipation? I didn't know, but I continued, sliding the strap through the buckle until snug. I pulled until a hole caught the stem of the buckle, which was a little tighter than at first. The collar relaxed the hold a little when I had finished with the clasp.

So here I stood with a collar around my neck. My breathing skyrocketed. Too tight? No, wasn't tight at all, just snug. Is this what I would feel every day? When the image flashed in my mind, a dull ache sprouted, not in my belly, but in my vagina. He said a collar could be erotic. Arousal or fear? I don't know. Fear can be an aphrodisiac. I do know if Jordan walked in the door, I would be all over him. Then he would be mad, because he told me I couldn't give the submissive thing a trial run. Dammit.

I'm so fucked up.

Natural fabrics, cotton, wool, and silk surround your skin each with a unique texture. Leather had its own special smooth coolness, and flaccidity. Each breath I took with my throat expanding against the band counted down from panic to calm, and I wasn't quite as afraid. Because Jordan said he wanted our moment of collaring to be special, I should have taken the thing off, but I didn't. I wanted to know what extended wear would be like so I wore the collar all evening. The feeling of the leather strap around my neck kind of drove me crazy, not in a frightening way. I kept tugging, even though the tugging did absolutely nothing but say, "Yes, I'm still attached." After a few hours, the need to masturbate consumed me. This collar thing had me going off in record time. Even after satisfying myself, I was wet all freakin' night.

After hours of tossing in bed and getting myself off two more times, I collapsed into an exhausted slumber. The next morning, when I awoke, I didn't even realize I still wore the collar until I caught a glimpse at myself in the mirror. In a few hours during the night, I had adjusted to the feel of what could very well be my future.

Two days later, I was waiting at Jordan's condo door when he arrived home. When he saw me, his face became both surprised and happy simultaneously.

"Hi. And to what do I owe the pleasure?" he said wrapping his arms around me.

"I want to marry you and everything that comes with it," I said a little breathless and shocked I spoke these words. Jordan remained silent. I couldn't read his usually vivid face. He'd changed his mind, and now my excitement turned to nausea.

He had changed his mind.

"Angel, you have to be sure. Are you?" His eyes changed from ice to dark blue and his face read apprehensive instead of happy.

I was sure until then. "Yes," I said, but not with the conviction, I possessed earlier. "Have you changed your mind about wanting to marry me?"

He hugged me tight into his chest. "No. No, Angel. I haven't changed my mind. I love you. I just want you to be sure."

Chapter Five

Jessica had been chewing on the end of the pen for the last several minutes. The action was a little annoying, but when you are trying to convince someone who is writing about your life that it is not weird or perverted, best not to piss her off.

"What was your wedding like?" she asked.

"Like everyone else's. I mean we could have had this huge wedding at the cathedral and reception at the Indiana Club, but we chose to have a more intimate setting with close family and friends. The whole day was all very relaxed and loads of fun. We flew to Jamaica for a week then came home and started our lives."

"So were you wearing the collar at the ceremony?"

"No. That didn't happen until after we were home."

****

What I viewed of Jamaica was fabulous. My most exquisite memories of Jamaica were of our suite by the ocean, and what I experienced most of was the king-sized bed and Jordan on top, under and at both ends of me. I was so exhausted during our honeymoon, going back to work was like vacation. I can't deny our honeymoon was the most incredible experience of my life. I learned so much about my body from Jordan unlocking every secret of how to introduce me to a new life—waking up the sexual entity inside of me.

The Friday after we returned from our honeymoon, I left work a little early, but found Jordan had already arrived at home. Before the wedding, we agreed whoever arrived home first would start dinner. I walked in to smells of sizzling steaks. Perfect for the still cold April evening. I was even thinking about making s'mores in front of the fireplace.

"Hi," He opened the broiler to flip the New York Strips. The potatoes and salad are ready. Just need to wait on the steaks. How was your day?"

"Fine. You must have left work earlier than I did to be this far along with dinner. The steaks smell wonderful, and I'm starving. I didn't eat lunch."

"And why not?" he asked.

"Too busy."

"That's crazy. You need to eat. I'll come and take you to lunch every day if that is what I have to do." He laughed, but I was sure he was serious.

"I know. I just wanted to find a good stopping point so I could hurry home to you?"

He kissed my forehead. "Good move. Flattery will get you places."

We enjoyed the steak dinner on the floor in front of the fire. I thought to gather our plates when were finished, but Jordan stopped me. "I'll get these. I want you to go take a shower."

"Why?" I asked.

"We're going to start tonight. So no shower in the morning. And would you put on the nightgown you wore on our wedding night."

I was standing, but Jordan remained on the floor. He touched my hand. "Go, on, Angel, I'll be in soon."

So, tonight. I agreed. I said I wanted this, but now, I was terrified. Somehow, I believed since we had been home a week and he had not mentioned anything, a part of me considered or maybe wished he might have changed his mind.

Walking to the bedroom transformed into the last mile. Every action to remove my clothes I watched in slow motion. My hands, feet, and shoulders were heavy with the imminent change in my life.

I let the hot water run over me, until the spray turned cold driving me from the safety of the shower to Jordan waiting in our bedroom. Always a patient man, but still a man who had a limit to how much his wife could test him.

When I opened the shower door, I could see he had put fresh towels on the sink and flowing from a hanger on the door was the black silk long gown I wore our first night in Jamaica. The low-cut front and even lower-cut back showed a lot of skin, but still covered enough to be seductive. He said he loved how hot I looked wearing the gown, and I loved how confident I became as soon as the silk glided along the contours of my body. The little things he remembered triggered a smile—boosting my resolve, my conviction.

I toweled off, slipped into the gown ready to make the biggest change in my life ever.

Jordan stood into the middle of our bedroom dressed in just navy blue lounge pants. His bare chest with the tattoo glaring in my face made my heart pound. With the lock of hair hung over his forehead after sleeping, I kept thinking how lucky I was to have this man. He was handsome, sweet, smart, and had a big secret. He let me know his secret, asked me to join him. I had given him my heart, my soul, my love, and now he would have my body in a way I believed expressed I belonged to one man.

I approached a new life, wrapping my arms around his waist, laying my head on his chest to feel his heartbeat, pounding as intensely as mine was. My head fit perfectly under his chin, and he kissed the top of my head while he played with my still damp hair winding the mass of dark curls on top of my head before he secured the waves with a clip.

"Turn around, Angel."

His hand never left my skin, gliding along my shoulders as I turned my back. I started to tremble. I knew what was coming, and I was scared.

When he placed his other hand on my shoulder, the smooth leather of the collar brushed my left shoulder, and I flinched. He kissed my neck, swirling his tongue at its base. The tremble turned into a shiver. I wanted him. I wanted him inside me so much. He stopped the kissing, and my eyes caught a tiny glimpse as he drew the not-even-an inch wide black collar to my neck. I swallowed several times. My rapid breathing made me light-headed. I leaned back so Jordan's body could steady me a little.

"It's okay, Angel. Whatever you need. Just lean on me," he whispered.

Then the smoothness of the leather touched my skin. I flinched even more as he pulled the end to the buckle. A little at a time he tightened to his satisfaction I suppose. Though not loud, the slight jingle of the metal clasp sounded like clanging symbols in my ears.

I belonged to my husband.

I couldn't stop the tears running down my cheek.

My life now changed forever. I kept telling myself I wanted this, and Jordan would guide me. His thumb tried brushing the tears away, but they kept falling. He gave up, and instead wrapped his arms around me. I turned into his bare chest inhaling his scent as he rested his chin on top of my head. "You are going to have to help me, Jordan," I managed to say between sniffles.

"Angel, I'll always be here to help you." He broke our embrace to sling his arm around my shoulder. "Let's go lie in the bed."

Lying in the bed wrapped in Jordan's arms, I came to grips with what I had agreed to, and the change encircling my neck wasn't bad. He was right. Somewhere between the tears and his embrace, discomfort materialized between my legs, but uncomfortable in a good way. The impulses from the snugness of the collar had shimmied down to my clit.

"Jordan? Will you touch me?" I asked.

"No, Angel. Not right now. Not because I don't want to, but you'll have to wait.

I let out a disappointed sigh, and a feather light kiss brushed my forehead before I drifted off to sleep.

I woke up Saturday morning to the smell of bacon and coffee. My tech-trained brain awoke, and I rolled over to check the clock on my phone—seven thirty. I guess I'd been exhausted. The last time I checked, the time read nine and I must have fell asleep somewhere around that time. As I stretched, my hand brushed the collar. Less than twelve hours after he secured our bond, and just like my own trial, I barely registered the presence of the collar. However, when I touched the surface again, a familiar ache started to build between my legs. Was I so horny because of a simple strip of leather or was the sensation because Jordan wouldn't have sex with me last night.

I assumed both.

Instead of trying to deal with my tangled mass of hair, I went straight to the kitchen, finding Jordan at the stove. His ass filled out the navy lounge pants, and I just wanted to touch the skin beneath the black T-shirt stretching across his back.

"Hi," I said through a yawn.

He turned around. His messed up, too long hair started to make me squirm all over again. I wasn't going to last much longer. "Hungry?" he asked.

Hell yes, I was hungry, but not for bacon. "Sure." I opened the cabinet, chose a mug, and helped myself to coffee, all the while watching him transfer the dripping bacon from the skillet to a waiting plate lined with paper towels. The flexing of his biceps as he handled the skillet, the way his shoulders stretched the seams from his shirt, the morning hair all made cooking bacon the sexiest thing I'd ever witnessed. "One egg or two," he asked, cracking one into the pan.

"Just one," I said, then taking a sip of the coffee, my eyes never leaving his ass.

"Since when do you like coffee?" he asked.

I didn't, but I experimented with the notion the bitterness might take my mind off my oohoo itch.

Didn't work. "I thought I'd try again. Since you're good at cooking and other things, I considered maybe you made great coffee." I sipped the bitter liquid again. "You don't."

"I make excellent coffee." His icy blues narrowed at me. "There is something clinically wrong with a person who doesn't like coffee."

"There is something wrong with a person who is leading someone else on by looking like an orgasm making machine and not allowing someone any relief."

Instead of answering, Jordan grabbed two plates from the cabinet and dished up our breakfast. He handed me my plate and said. "Go sit down and eat."

He didn't seem angry or amused or anything. He carried his own plate to the table, while I stood with my mouth open until he said. "Come have breakfast with me."

I joined him at the table with a little trepidation. My collar squeezed my neck. The lump in my throat may have been the culprit. Without a word, I started eating the bacon and scrambled eggs. "Did I say something wrong?" I asked a little afraid of his answer.

"Not at all." Then he winked. "I'm just trying to decide when you get some relief. Go get dressed when you finish."

"Dressed?" I asked.

"Yes."

"We're going out?" I wasn't ready to go out. I may never be ready to go outside our home. Everyone would know the minute I stepped into the world.

"Yes, we're going out. There is a street festival in Irvington today. It's not going to be as cold today. We're going out. You have to be able to go out."

"I know, but already?"

"You'll be fine."

When I finished, I carted both plates to the sink. "I need to shower," I told him.

"You showered last night. I want you to wait until tomorrow."

"But my hair," I protested.

"Your hair is fine. Kind of wild angel like. Just go get dressed."

"Are you going to shower?"

"Of course I am," he replied.

"How is that fair?"—not realizing I said the words aloud. Bad habit of mine.

"I didn't shower last night, and fair does not enter into the equation today." He winked at me. *Dammit, stop doing that.* My pussy equivalent of a massive hard on was getting a little painful.

Although my heavy exaggerated sigh was loud enough for him to hear, he said nothing so I trudged to my closet in the spare bedroom. Jordan and I had shopped to buy clothes to hide the collar, but at the time, this new chapter lived in the surreal and would never happen. Today, I would go out in public attempting to hide my new secret, and I was terrified.

I rifled through my choices, finally deciding on a pale pink cashmere turtleneck and a gray denim short skirt. The April weather was still cold enough for the outfit, so my ensemble didn't scream "Hey, look at the virgin submissive." I draped a pink and gray plaid cotton scarf around the back of my neck for an extra measure of safety. Then to be even more secure, I shrugged into a short-waist black leather jacket with a stand up collar I left unzipped. To finish, I added a pair of black ankle boots with three-inch heels.

The hair, well my hair was another thing. I didn't use a blow dryer after showering last night, so this morning, wave upon wave upon wave greeted me. Gathering my hair behind my head, I secured the dark mass of curls into a ponytail, extracting a few of the brown ringlets to frame my face. Mascara, lipstick, and

I was ready.

Scanning myself in the full-length mirror, I checked myself three times; wanting to be sure I could completely pull off this masquerade of kink. When I walked into the kitchen, Jordan put down his coffee. He was showered, shaved, and as usual made me feel like Cinderella's ugly stepsister. "Damn," he said. "You're so fuckin' hot. I almost want to stay here."

"I'd be okay with the change in plans," I said.

He turned my hand to kiss my palm. "I am taking my beautiful wife out for the day, and she will be perfectly fine."

I swallowed and felt the pressure of the collar in more ways than one.

****

Jordan did pick a nice place for us to go on this first day of my public collaring. I loved Irvington. The small historic community oozed with architectural beauties. The homes ranged from Victorian Gothic, Colonial Revival, Tudor, and Arts and Crafts, but what was fascinating was most of the homes in Irvington were considered haunted. Almost everyone I had talked with who lived in Irvington had a ghost story to tell which included the Lincoln Ghost Train and the notorious H.H. Holmes, the notorious serial killer during the Chicago World's Fair. He committed one of his last murders in Irvington.

The tree-lined streets, cafes, eclectic shops, and numerous festivals attracted a wide-range of visitors. Today's festival was a mixture of art, crafts, and artisan foods. A blues band played a lyrical tune. The sun was out. The wind was brisk, and here I was about to piss myself with the fear of being discovered.

Little by little, I relaxed. I wasn't being scrutinized or even stared at by the hundreds of strangers who crossed our path. However, I was concentrating on walking a few steps behind Jordan. I read on a website when in public, some submissives are often required to walk steps behind their Dominant. About fifteen minutes into our stroll through the vendor booths, I lost my balance as Jordan yanked me into his body.

In a low but stern whisper, he said. "I know what you are doing, and I want you to stop." Those eyes of blues were intense, but not angry. He put his finger in line with my nose. "And stay off those damn submissive internet sites."

When we started walking again, I made sure each step matched his, but so did his hand as he grasped mine tightly interlacing our fingers. His little gesture of control didn't make me angry. Not at all. I was excited.

One of the artists' booths grabbed both of our attention. The acrylics of city life and the downtown skyline were mesmerizing. The canal walk, the stadium, the river, the state's oldest bar bloomed to life in the artist's rendering.

"I think we need to get something for the condo," he said.

"You already have some nice artwork," I said.

"Yes, but we need something that is ours, not just mine. Which one do you like?"

I perused the paintings hanging all around the canvas-roofed booth. There were so many talking to me, deciding was difficult. However, one screamed my name. I stepped to the middle of the masterpiece to see the detail. The view was of the city skyline from the pedestrian bridge between the zoo and museum campus park. By the bridge railing, stood a couple arm in arm staring at the skyline in the twilight. The women's head lay upon the man's shoulder. From the back, the couple could have been Jordan and me. "This one," I said. "I love this one."

I smiled when familiar hands squeezed my shoulders.

"It's perfect for us," he said.

I almost choked when I glanced at the price. Fifteen hundred dollars. "I don't know. That's a lot of money. I mean it's beautiful and all, but kind of expensive."

"I know, but we need something we both have a connection to in our home." He stepped away from me to the artist. I could not hear what they were saying, but Jordan pointed to the painting. The artist grinned and left his stool to retrieve the painting. "Ah, yes, this one is special," the artist said. "Very peaceful. I think you two'll be very happy."

Jordan paid with his credit card, and while we waited for the artist to wrap the painting in brown paper for us to carry, Jordan kissed the top of my head.

The artist took his time wrapping the painting, carefully placing each section of the paper around the work. "This work is one of my favorites. You two could be the couple. Newlyweds?"

"Yes," Jordan replied. "A few weeks now."

"Well, you are a lucky man." The artist winked at me.

I think I blushed a little. *I think I'm pretty lucky, too. What woman wouldn't want to wake up next to Jordan with his thing poking you in the back?*

The picture was sofa size, making the piece

awkward to carry, but Jordan tucked our painting under his arm as we strolled on to other booths. After an hour, I needed a break. "Can I get something to drink?" I asked.

His stop was so abrupt; I'd swear he'd walked into an invisible brick wall. Since English is my only language, and I don't stutter, I know he heard what I said. However, the arcing eyebrows and subsequent glare stopped me in my own tracks while I pondered either his confusion or irritation.

"Sure." He turned away for a moment. "Go get something to drink, and then come across the street to the park. I'll wait at a table."

At that moment, the tables were empty of people, but in an hour or so, festivalgoers wanting to eat would fill them. As I waited to get lemonade, I followed Jordan's path to the isolated picnic table he had chosen resting under a towering ancient oak tree. An uneasy sensation crept through me when the girl handed me the lemonade and popcorn.

Something was off.

When I shuffled hesitantly to where Jordan sat, I set the lemonade and popcorn bag on the table. I started to sit beside Jordan, but he grabbed my waist and set me into his lap with my back to the crowd.

"Did I do something wrong?" The smell of the popcorn started my stomach reeling.

He brushed the loose tendril from my face. "In a way."

My stomach hit the ground. I wasn't even aware. I had no clue what I did.

"Angel, when I fell in love with you…"
Oh, shit. This is bad.

"…I fell in love with you. You as you were. Your openness, your sense of humor, your silliness. Angel, I want you to be you. Not what you think I want you to be. Not what you've read on a web site. Everyone who is in a relationship like ours is different. We all want different things. This part of life is not cookie cutter. It's not all of the same protocol."

I surveyed the stitching in my skirt trying to fight back the tears. I hated being a crier. "I just don't know what to do."

"Look at me." He paused until I looked up. "I want you to always look at me when you talk." My head and heart feared what I would see in his eyes. They changed so much with his mood, but now, they were warm and soothing.

"I really haven't told you a lot about my past living in the scene as a Dominant, because I'm still a little conflicted. We'll talk more when we get home, but right now, I want to say this. I do want control over you…in the bedroom, not out here. Not at your job. Not in everyday life. Yes. I want you to wear this collar as a reminder you're for me. You're everything to me. And when I do this…"

His left hand shimmied up my skirt, slipping under my panties, inching their way to my slit. I tensed. *Oh, shit. Not here. Not here.*

His right hand burrowed under the fold of the turtleneck. He caressed the collar through the cashmere. *Oh shit again.* The slight pressure on the collar combined with the sneaky little finger trick in my vagina was making me very uncomfortable and tense.

"Jordan, you, you, you have t-t-too stop." My rapid breathing impeded my ability to talk.

"Shh. No one can see us."

"Someone might see us. I can't do that, and you know I can't keep quiet," I said.

He continued with the motions, adding a chaste kiss to the mix, but the pressure grew as he increased his massage on my neck and clit.

Oh dear God, I'm going to have a fuckin' orgasm right here in the historic district.

Then he stopped. *What?*

His left hand abandoned me. If my clit had a hand, fingers would have grabbed his and said "not so fast, mister. Get back here."

I didn't appreciate the amused snicker from the purposeful man. He broke the kiss with a Cheshire cat grin.

"You're a real bastard," I said. "You're aware, right?"

"Ahh. There's she is." He kissed my forehead, and then picked up the lemonade. "I promise. We will have another talk when we get home."

"Just talk?"

"We'll see."

"That's what my dad always said. 'We'll see' always meant 'no'."

He laughed and then offered me the lemonade I had forgotten while his hand roamed underneath my skirt.

****

Jessica leaned her back against the sofa. She blinked rapidly like the flickering of an old movie, and I could tell she had so many images flashing in her head, so I just let her process them before we continued. She set the laptop aside. "May I use the restroom?" she asked.

"Sure. Second door on the left."

She stood and stretched before making her way toward the bathroom. Instead, though, she stopped at the bedroom door, taking the knob and twisting. Thank God, my husband had locked it from the inside. "The *second* door, I said."

"I'm sorry, I didn't mean to. I wasn't paying attention," she apologized.

I'm not completely stupid. I know she was trying to *accidently* open the door to see if anyone was on the other side. She was a journalist, and doing her job, I suppose, trying to find the truth. Not today.

When she returned, she stopped right behind the loveseat. "Oh, what a lovely tattoo. What's its significance, if you don't mind my asking?"

Shit. When I removed the sweater, I forgot about the tattoo on my left shoulder. The angel-wing design was small, just about two inches tall, with initials intertwined on the inside where the wings met. Other than the C, the letters were barely discernible. I changed my mind three times, and on the way to the tattoo parlor, I now wished I'd changed my mind for the fourth and final time, but I didn't. I didn't consider what a tat looks like on an eighty-year-old woman with wrinkly skin. Now though, like many, I regretted getting the tattoo—a silly and expensive whim.

"My grandmother and I were very close."

"Are those letters inside the wings? I can't quite make them out."

"Carol was her name." I was getting way too good at being a liar. My father's mother had died when he was a kid, and her name was Selma, not Carol. My grandma Cindy had passed as well. She was a fine grandma, but I would never get a tattoo in her honor.

"What a wonderful way to honor her," Jessica said as she returned to the love seat. "When you said your husband was going to talk more about what your role was when you got home, did you talk more?"

"He did, but not at first…

****

Jordan was happy to put down the cumbersome painting. I kept waiting for our discussion to resume. I waited awhile.

"Go get undressed, and I'll take that off so you can shower," he said.

I was more excited about being able to shower than taking off the collar. I was beginning to understand and like the effect on me. Jordan walked into the bedroom when I unhooked my bra. Without a word, he stood behind me to unbuckle the collar. With every brush stroke of his finders on my neck, waves of hot shocks raced up and down my desperate body. His feel-up at the park still lingered, and I turned around, putting my arms around his neck.

"I had a nice day," I said.

"We did. I think the painting is important for us to have, and important for you to know you can be out and everything is fine."

He began rubbing my naked back. Oh my God, his fingers were magic, alternating raking my skin with his fingertips to massaging his thumbs up and down my spine. I shifted my body closer to rip his shirt out of his pants. The intoxicating massage screeched to a halt as strong hands clamped around my wrists.

I screamed. Internally, but still I screamed.

"Jordan?" with a maybe a hint of a whine "Throw me a bone, please, something."

"I thought you wanted to take a shower?" Nothing but amusement sparkled in his eyes.

"I do, desperately, but I'm a little more desperate for something else," *Did that sound like begging?*

"I do love it when you beg," he said with big smile on his face.

Damn. I was begging. That's never good.

"Go take a shower first, and then we'll see."

"We'll see. Again, I know the meaning." Bare feet don't emit much noise stopping, but I did my best. Once in the shower, with steaming water pelleting my skin, some of my tension melted away. I know Jordan wasn't being mean or rejecting me. He was teaching me patience and control which would help me accept this life. So far, my failure rate teetered on one hundred percent. I was so wound up, I was ready to explode, and when the green flag dropped for sex, God help him, I would be insanely out of control.

By the time I finished with my shower, I was a little calmer. Nothing like being clean to help you process your day.

My day. I walked around in public with a leather collar around my neck hoping no one pointed to the weird acting girl, all the while being somewhere between being horny as hell and terrified. Add to the list my hot-as-hell husband driving me insane with his sexual taunting, dangling at the end of the carrot I believed I never would get.

Wrapping a towel around my body, I went to the spare bedroom where most of my clothes were in the closet and dresser.

Picking through the underwear drawer, I chose then discarded each pair I picked up. I don't know why, but somehow today my underwear resembled granny pants. I should have bought new underwear before we got married. I settled on the black silky ones Jordan had purchased for me on one of the weekends I had stayed over, before were married.

As I had them in my hand, damn, I was wet again remembering how Jordan touched me in all the right places, never letting me touch him until I was screaming with the need to release. I should have known then what he was doing, but I was too obsessed with every inch of this man to notice I was already submitting.

My reminiscing came to a screeching halt as Jordan grabbed me from behind. I screamed. The towel dropped to the floor. He scooped me up and carried me to the bedroom all before I could process what just happened. He stood next to the bed holding me over the top.

My heart raced right along with his. The feel of his bare chest against my breast made my nipples salute. He had on boxers, but his cock was like a snake ready to strike.

"You're just going to fuck with me instead of fucking me, aren't you," I asked him, catching a whiff of his aftershave.

His gaze was no longer jovial. "The first new rule in here is the language goes away."

Not one ounce of teasing crossed his chilling stare. "Okay," I whispered.

He dropped me into the middle of the bed and pounced over the top of me capturing my wrists with his hands and assaulting my lips with his. The low growl from the back of his throat propelled an involuntary response to my legs, wrapping them around his waist to force his package much closer to pay dirt.

"Slow down, Angel. We have all night, and I intend to use every minute."

Oh, damn. I devoured the air surrounding us—just his ocean and sand scent was enough to get me wet. As soon as he released my hands, they were all over his back. In turn, Jordan reacted with his own deep inhale, but just as he did, he whispered in my ear. "You keep forgetting in here, I'm in charge."

"I want you inside of me," I said in a ragged breath. His hours of teasing me had literally put me in pain, and if I didn't get some release soon, I would surely die.

"We'll get there, Angel. We'll get there. Here, take my hands." He intertwined our fingers and plunged our hands forward, and closer to the headboard. He nibbled the hollow of my neck and said in a husky tone, "Grab the rails. Don't let go, no matter what."

I let go of the hands whose touch always made me feel safe and grabbed hold of the rod iron vertical rails on the headboard. The cold metal chilled me all through my body. The "no matter what" concerned me. The fear enveloping me made my body tremble with the anticipation of what was to come.

I was never afraid of *him*. This was a fear I couldn't do what he asked. When Jordan touched me, the magical explosion of fireworks he created inside of me were so intense—I didn't think I could finish this test—a test to watch me struggle to release all control—the ultimate trial of my trust.

I didn't trust myself. Having Jordan on top of me and not being able to touch him was like setting a whole chocolate cake in my lap and telling me if I didn't take a bite, I may or may not get to eat a piece. Preposterous and cruel. However, in the spirit of agreeing to let my husband be the master in the bedroom, I was going to white-knuckle it through this.

He stepped away just long enough to drop his boxers, coming back to me, slipping his arms underneath my back, taking my right nipple deep inside his mouth. He licked, sucked, and bit hard enough I cried out from the pain shooting ultimate lashes of ecstasy through my body, and I was unable to breathe. I only caught a breath, when he released my nipple to trace a jagged path with his tongue down my middle to my navel, circling its rim before moving on.

The rails rattled every time I had to tighten my grip. Two breaths—one ragged and one calm—cut through the silent room. But with every breath I exhaled, the new one rested in my lungs far longer than natural.

He slid his hands farther down to cup my butt signally where he intended to land. I failed again to breathe as he kissed my slit with a feather soft sensation. He kissed and suckled again, again, and again. I still wasn't breathing.

"Breathe, Angel. You have to breathe."

"I can't," I squeaked.

"Breathe or I'll stop."

He stopped.

I inhaled like a drowning woman.

Oh, air—so much better. I may not have patience, but I was becoming exceptional at holding my breath.

Jordan shifted his focus from my oohoo back to my breasts. For years, I wasn't a fan of booby biting, but something about his tongue and perfect teeth pretty much just made me want to shove them in his mouth all of the time, kind of like a tittycicle without the possibility of melting.

An effortless transition from immersing my breasts in liquid heat to grazing my hairline with stinging nips injected a paralyzing drug throughout my body. "You like?" he whispered in my ear.

Was I allowed to speak or not? A neutral low encouraging moan did the trick. The bites got harder. The moans louder. All the while, he was devouring my nipples and neck, Jordan's fingers were sliding in and out of me, kneading my clit. He pulled them out, and then inserted his dripping wet fingers into my mouth. "Taste how sweet you are," he whispered.

Didn't really taste like anything, but who was I to argue in a situation where my flavor was the least of my concerns.

Oh my God! "Jordan, please, please." I needed to release.

"Hold on, Baby. Control yourself, Angel, until I tell you." Even his velvety smooth voice did little to ease my torture.

He returned his fingers, sliding back into my secret place. He kissed my forehead, and then licked my lips before entering my mouth with his tongue. The rhythm of his fingers increased, as did his force on my lips. His own moaning was driving me to the edge.

"Come on Angel, come for me. Come for me."

Thank God. "Oh Hell yes. Shit." *Language. Language. Really how does he expect me not to cuss when he's doing delicious deeds to my body?*

As the waves of my orgasm crashed, Jordan plunged deep into me, thrusting harder and beyond what I assumed existed. And when the pressure began to build all over again—still I clutched the rails. Right before his own explosion, he wrapped his arms around me. His teeth clamped down on my neck just beneath my jaw. The sudden, sharp, and eye-opening bite caused me to cry out, but gratification erased any pain. He meant to mark me, and I reveled in the idea of bearing his brand.

He collapsed on me, forcing the air from my lungs with a whoosh. Jordan's not a huge, bulky guy, but he's tall and heavy and sprawled all over my body, but I loved the pressure. The fact I couldn't budge an inch when he was on me, was a restraint I couldn't get enough of.

He got up to retrieve his boxers. "Are you okay?"

I gave him a slight nod.

"I don't have my contacts in. I can't see what you're doing. You have to talk to me."

"You can see me. I know you can see without your contacts." As long I still had a heartbeat, things were good. Right now, my heart rhythm sounded like a steel drum band. This talk, no talk thing was confusing.

"You need to speak to me, not just motions." He flopped on the bed. "And let go of the rails."

"Yes," I said. "I'm okay." finger by finger, I peeled away my grip. Deep red indentions branded my hands.

He left the room but returned with one of my nightshirts—my favorite soft, silky black chemise with enough material to cover my butt, but not if I raised my hands. "Here put this on so we can talk."

I slipped the comfortable shirt over my head before moving to sit on the edge of the bed. Jordan sat beside me. "Hold your hair up, please."

I gathered my hair, holding the mass high on my head, as the second arrival of my new calling blurred the patterns of the landscape hanging on the wall. I closed my eyes when the defining leather of purpose enclosed my neck. He passed the end through the buckle pulling the strap to destination and destiny. I swallowed from a pressure more than yesterday. A small wave of panic grew inside of me. "Jordan?" I whispered.

"Yesterday was adjusting. You'll be okay. Just relax. In a few minutes, you'll be fine."

He kissed my jaw. With each rapid breath, I was trying to quell the panic. Then the panic ebbed away— replaced with a joy, a euphoria, a tightening in my groin as if a new person emerged from a Sleeping Beauty existence. I embraced the awareness of my body's reaction to this simple piece of leather. I liked the consciousness of my sexuality rising. This piece of leather was changing everything I deemed true about myself.

I couldn't relax, because now I was so turned on, I just wanted Jordan inside of me again "Can we?"

"Can we what?" he asked. His eyes so blue right now.

"Mess the sheets up again."

Jordan let out a huge laugh, reclined on the bed, pulling me with him. "You're getting a little insatiable, aren't you?"

"Not until you came along." I replied.

"Not now. Here sit up. We're going to talk some

more."

I rolled over and crawled to the middle of the bed, while Jordan followed, but instead of sitting beside me, he placed me sideways in his lap. He began combing his fingers through my hair as I lay my head against his chest, listening to the rhythm of his heart. The steady and strong rhythm was calming to my nervousness about our talk.

He touched my collar. "You know why I wanted you to wear this, don't you?"

I inhaled a deep breath recalling our earlier conversations. "You want me to always know I'm yours and you're forever part of me."

"Yes, but it's something else, too. When you wear this, you have my promise you're always first in my life. Nothing else comes before what you need. I'll always be there for you, no matter what. Do you understand what I'm saying? How do you feel?"

"I wasn't prepared for how horny this makes me. I'm still really scared about going out in public."

"No one will notice."

"I knew you would respond to being dominated. I say that, but what I mean is I know you want me to lead you, to guide you when we're having sex. It's a turn on for you. Your brain and body are relating the collar to our sexual time."

I acknowledged what he was saying internally, but I didn't respond. I couldn't argue something so true. Never had a man fulfilled me as deeply as Jordan had, and he was making all of the decisions. Everyone was on point. When the day arrived for my first bondage experience, I didn't know if I would be able to handle the feeling of intensity I believed was coming.

As if he read my mind, He stopped caressing my hair to hug me. "When we do a scene, you won't be scared. Like the collar, the restraints will give you a tremendous feeling of sexual awareness and arousal. Sometimes, you might be uncomfortable, but never will I hurt you, and if it gets to be too much, you can always say so, and we'll stop. Never be afraid to tell me to stop. I'll keep reminding you. I think if you're ready, we can experiment a little tomorrow. Nothing too extreme."

Still with my head on his chest, I let out a heavy sigh of uncertainty. My internet research had so many images floating around in my head. Where did Jordan fit in these images? Some the web images I discovered were more freakish than arousing. Some were so extreme, I couldn't look at them for more than a few seconds, but some were intriguing, arousing, and beautiful.

His voice guided me back to reality. "About today. I must have given you an impression I want a certain protocol and obedience from you. I am sorry, because that's not me."

I listened but remained still. I think understanding his words was easier if I didn't watch his face. His face was distracting, in a good way, but his voice was mesmerizing. I'm sure one reason he was so good at his job was the hypnotizing melody of his voice. Every word was a lullaby to my heart.

"Angel, I don't want you to be less than me. I don't want you to walk behind me or ask me if you want a drink, food, or anything remotely close. I want you to watch me when we're talking and question me when you don't agree."

Now I had to say something, "But…" I didn't get far.

"With exception to when we are having sex or doing restriction. Then you listen and don't talk. Unless it's an emergency. Just let me do the talking."

"Why?"

"Because if you're talking, your focus is talking, not responding. I want your mind exploring and reacting to what I'm saying and not concentrating on what words you want to say. Which brings me to another point. I don't like to hear you cuss. Not at all. Everyday situations are a part of life. In here…no."

I nodded against his chest.

"Angel."

"Yes. You don't want to hear me cuss in the bedroom." My closed eyes popped open with a realization. "Wait a minute. I've heard you say stuff."

"I think you're mistaken." Jordan pulled a strand of my hair.

"No, I don't think so." I started to raise my head, but his hand forced my face into his chest.

"Yes, you are."

Whatever. I get it.

He kissed the top of my head. "Don't think for a minute I'll try and tell you what you should be doing in your career. I won't. You're the one who knows what's best for you. I love you, Angel. I love you like I didn't think I could love anyone, but I won't make the decisions you need to make. I'll give you my opinion if you want."

When he differentiated between the two lives, my soul began fusing with his body. We were one. When he first told me about what he wanted, I was shocked and scared, but now I grasped the concept this wasn't about control, but about extracting me out of me. I was still a little scared of what was to come, but curious and excited as well.

I wanted to know more.

"Jordan. I know you told me you stopped the Dominant lifestyle because it didn't suit you anymore, but you were vague. Will you tell me? What was your life like? And, why did you stop?"

He shifted our weight, absorbing more of mine. "There was no dancing around the subject. Like minds. This group I was in, not only talked about the practice, but we would meet regularly to have parties, called play parties. There, you would meet other people who were interested, and sometimes there would be like a class or demonstration about certain scenes. It was fun and exciting. Sex or bondage and no attachments. I believed I'd found everything I wanted."

I was getting a little uncomfortable with the information, but I asked and Jordan was always up front with what he said. "Did you ever have women here or just at the parties."

"I lived in another apartment. The extra bedroom I used for those activities and for them to sleep there. When I made the decision to step away, I moved here. So, no, none of those women have ever been here."

Relied flooded through me with what I needed to hear. "You never slept in the same room with them?" I asked. Not sleeping together...how odd.

"Sometimes, but often in a Dom/sub relationship, the sub sleeps in a separate space. It keeps sub in the proper stature. I know this sounds awful to you. But, no one is coerced. It's all consensual. However, some of the things important to many of the subs, I wasn't comfortable with."

His caresses lulled my senses to the edge of sleep, but I wanted to know more.

"I was never comfortable with the sub kneeling before me. The nature of the BDSM life can be hundreds of different ways and is as individual as what flavor of ice cream you like. And I couldn't find one flavor to suit me."

He squeezed me tighter, kissing the top of my head, warming me all over.

"A lot of the subs I knew, well, were really into the pain for pleasure aspect, and a lot of the Dominants delivered, but I couldn't. I couldn't whip or spank a woman, nor discipline, causing them so much pain in order to get them aroused. When I couldn't deliver to them, they would go to someone who could. After enough disappointment and frustration, I realized I wasn't whole-heartedly into the scene, but internally I still had this desire."

I raised my head to his handsome face with his messed up hair falling over his forehead. "I didn't know I had a need, but I guess I do. I have never felt so secure or satisfied or even satiated."

"I'm not so sure you are satiated," he said with a smile.

His hand found my hair again, stroking the long strands from top to bottom, and I fought the sleep begging me to succumb. "Angel, I'll do many things to you, but I can only do them if you trust me completely. I'm doing them for you, as well as me. You're my joy. I know right now, you don't understand what all of this means, but I promise you, you'll feel things you've never dreamed of."

"I never dreamed it would be like this." I scrambled to sit, catching my hair in his hand. "Ow." We managed to untangle enough for me to straddle him. When his hand rested on my waist, I shifted it to my lips, kissing his palm, then fingertips before I sucked his thumb as deep as I could. His hands were large, but always like velvet when he touched me.

"When you first told me you wanted me to wear this—" My free hand snapped to the collar "—I cried after you drove me home. I cried for hours. All of the fantastic times we had together, I was waiting for the ball to drop because everything about you appeared just right, like you were what I wanted and needed. So, there just had to be something wrong with you, and your confession was a doozy, I thought at first."

My words were making Jordan uncomfortable. I could tell by the feel of the tense tremors convulsing throughout his body, but he had to know what he asked of me was extremely unexpected, not to mention a lot left of center.

"After I stopped crying, I started to think. You could have just waited until after we got married to tell me, but doing so would have been wrong of you, and one thing I do know, you have a lot of integrity. Then I wondered, well why didn't you say something earlier on, but you were right, I would have ended the relationship and not have even gotten to know you. And right or wrong, I went to the internet. I know there's a lot of bad info there, but I had a starting point. I found a personal blog of a submissive, and I read like two years' worth of her blog in one night. My head was about to explode, but I wanted to know more...from you."

His tense muscles uncoiled a bit. "Here, you need to move your legs. Your knees are gonna hurt." With a huff, I severed the warm connection and shifted so I had wrapped my legs around his waist to balance myself and alert his pecker.

"I am endlessly grateful you chose to be with me. I know this wasn't an easy decision. I don't know why I'm this way. I didn't have a fucked up childhood. My life was all very normal. You've met my parents and my sister. There is nothing weird or perverted about them. Most of the people, who are in to this, are very normal. We just like to explore a different side of our desires."

"What'll we do tomorrow?" I asked. Part of me wanted to know, but there was an unstoppable fear. Silly maybe. I know Jordan wouldn't hurt me, but still…

He bent his knees, moving me more on his stomach than his now very erect penis. "Very light bondage. Just some tying up. Introductory course to see how you handle it."

"Bondage 101?"

He cocked his head with a throaty laugh. "A good a name as any, I suppose."

I wandered around the cavalcade of my stored memories for a few seconds. "This is different than what I thought. Here with you, I know what I want, what I was missing. Funny. I was missing something I didn't even know about."

"One more thing," he said.

"What?" I wasn't sure I could retain all of this. My mind kept flying around the room like a witch with a faulty broom.

"Saturday mornings are our time. You and me here. Make no plans other than being in here with me." Jordan latched onto a curl dangling in front of my face and twirled his finger in the spirals.

"What'll we be doing?" What could possibly be so important our Saturday morning calendar had to be clear?

"I don't know. A lot of things. Maybe nothing, but staying in bed watching TV. Doesn't matter. Just going to be us. No phones either."

His cock was rigid against my back. "Can I take care of this little problem behind me?"

"Little?" his eyes widened.

"Sorry, I misspoke." I unwrapped my legs from his waist, and before he could do or say anything, I stretched across the bed with my arm across his stomach and my mouth diving around his cock.

He wanted control, but right now, I wanted to show him what I could do. Repercussions be damned.

Chapter Six

Extraordinary loud stomach growling woke me on Sunday morning. We never left the bed the rest of the evening last night, so no dinner Saturday.

I rolled over to watch a still-asleep Jordan. *Damn.* How could life be so unjust he had eyelashes so long and thick? I know you are supposed to think your husband is hot, but mine was not only hot, but also downright beautiful, and a bit unnerving at times. He was easy going and light-hearted most of the time, but when the lights dimmed, and the door closed, he was serious and strong, but oh so smooth.

My intensive gaze must have penetrated his brain. Jordan opened his eyes. "What?" he said with a sleepy voice.

"Just looking," I said. "Wondering what you were going to make me for breakfast."

"What I'm going to make you for breakfast?"

"Is it my turn?" I teased.

"It's your turn." He flopped off to the other side. "Wake me up when we can eat."

I let out a sigh. "Would you like me to bring the plate to you in bed?"

"Hmmm?"

"You'll go hungry, if that's the case."

"I need to make more rules," he mumbled.

I hit him with a pillow, and then untangled my legs

from the sheets to start breakfast duty.

After breakfast, I was sure Jordan would want to go out again. I carried about a half an inch more confidence today than yesterday, but still worried someone would notice. We, or I should say, he wanted to walk from the condo through downtown and take in the ever-changing city.

We walked along the canal to the government office building before climbing to the street level to wander through the Wholesale District until we arrived on Massachusetts Avenue. Over the last several years, the street had evolved from a dangerous zone to the current "it" place of the city—hosting a myriad of restaurants, bars, and shops.

By then, the sun hit the midday sky, and my stomach requested attention. Fresh tacos and artisan margaritas made for a satisfying lunch.

I signaled to our server to order my third margarita, but Jordan stopped me. Now I'd acquired an alcohol monitor.

"I don't want you smashed for later, so no more. By the time we walk home, our food'll be settled, and we can do other things."

The phrase "other things," opened the curtain on "Jitters, the Musical." He possessed such an intuitive sense, he held out his hand across the table beckoning for my own shaking hand and injected unwavering reassurance deep in my veins. "Don't be nervous, Angel. It'll be fine. Better than fine."

As we walked home, Jordan clasped my hand, leading me to a new normal. Why did I feel like I was about to be led off to prison? Probably because I was closing a door on one way of life and entering another.

We talked about what all of this meant, but the reality was the classic fear of the unknown. What would he do to me? Could I handle what he gave? I trusted Jordan, right?

When I walked through the door I bolted to snatch a bottle of water. Really, I wanted a shot or two of rum, but Jordan had nixed my plans for being lit when the rope tying began.

At first, Jordan's calm exterior bothered me. He was so experienced, but today was kindergarten, and he was the teacher about to open the world to learning. Another idea rapped on my brain. If he showed any sign of being nervous, then panic loomed in my future. The only two times he showed me nerves was the night he told me he wanted to get married, and the other time was when he was putting the wedding ring on my finger.

As I slouched against the counter nursing the water, I eyed my husband's approach, following my gaze to his placement of tender hands on my shoulders. He had already changed. Well, he had taken off his shirt and was walking around in just jeans and bare feet. Fuck me he was hot.

"Sometime in this century when you finish your water, go get undressed, and wait for me on the bed."

I swallowed hard. The collar had already become so much a part of me, its presence assured rather than annoyed me. But now with every breath my new leather roommate reminded me something big was about to happen. He kissed me. Not hard, but just enough I wanted more. Jordan left to do God knows what. To find his little black bag of torture instruments I presumed.

The water bottle betrayed me, giving me my last sip. The water in my stomach betrayed me, trying to come up. *Stop it.* I needed to grow a pair and stop dawdling. I shuffled to the bedroom noticing he had set one of our dining room chairs at the end of the bed.

Scene of the crime.

Every shoe, sock, and other article of clothing I pulled off was edging me closer to our first lesson. I did a deep breathing exercise, but ten made me light-headed. After the world's longest and loneliest strip tease, I got down to just my black silky underwear.

I slipped into my white cotton shorty robe, for a bit more modesty until Jordan wanted me. I sat on the end of the bed, away from the chair, playing with imaginary lint when my trepidation arrived still without a shirt. Talk about a tease.

"You ready?" His voice, commanding but sensual, startled me from my over active imagination.

I nodded, but he continued to leer at me as if waiting for something. Oh yeah, the word thing. "Yes," I said without much conviction.

"Come here." He extended his hand. I stood believing I was ready, but maybe not. After all, he was my husband.

My hand trembled as I reached out. Dominant, but indulgent hands pulled a virgin submissive into his hard chest, kissing the top of my head. His eyes sparkled with amusement. No doubt at my hesitation or maybe the look of panic on my face.

He ripped the robe from my shoulders, exposing my bare breasts. "You are a fine angel. C'mere and sit down."

I shuffled my lead feet to the chair.

"Sit all of the way back," he said.

I know this was a bad analogy, but I wondered if this feeling of helplessness times a thousand filled condemned people when the guards arrived to get them. I mean I was excited to learn what he wanted to teach, but still, my fears stood steadfast.

I forced my back against the back of the chair, forcing my butt to the edge. My right knee bounced like I balanced a giggling baby on top. When my brain declared a cease and desist, my knee said, "Fuck you. This is how I deal."

Once again, complete quiet filled the room. I couldn't even hear the sound of my own breathing…because again, I'd stopped. For animals in the jungle, quiet meant danger lurked. By the watery scent I detected, someone dangerous prowled nearby.

Hot, directing, but tender lips kissed the side of my neck, calming me a microscopic proportion. Strands of his velvety hair brushed my cheek and tickled my nose. Draping his arm over my shoulder, he fondled my breast. Sliding my right nipple between his fingers did not help the nerves at all, but only shifted the tension elsewhere as my nipple grew taut beneath his firm touch.

He slipped around to my front, going to his knees, and the rope became visible—not thick, but rather thin, black and silky. He slid my right ankle to the outside of the chair leg, and then he wrapped the strand several times around my ankle and the chair leg.

As he wrapped more rope, his breathing increased with either excitement or nervousness…I didn't know. I did know hyperventilation might best describe my current breathing pattern.

After winding the rope to his satisfaction, he tied the knot. I couldn't flex my ankle a millimeter because he secured the rope tight enough to prevent any movement, but not enough to be painful. He repeated the process on my other leg. With my legs spread to publicly inappropriate, my vulnerability swallowed any calm or security I might have once possessed.

"Dammit," he gritted through his teeth, placing a hot sweaty hand on my knee. "You still have your underwear on. Why?"

"You didn't tell me to take them off."

Exasperated, I suppose exasperated best expressed his demeanor.

"I told you to get undressed."

"And I did. I left my underwear on, but I'm undressed. Besides. I'm not so sure about my bare ass on a chair. I don't know. Seems…well icky."

His hands curled into a fist and then out again. He let out one of those sighs interpreted as "really?" He stood, left the room, and returned with scissors in his hands.

"What are you going to do?" I didn't like any scenario, which included scissors and me tied to a chair.

He knelt before me. "I'm going to cut them off."

"Noooo. This is one of my few good pairs. You bought them for me," I wailed.

"The condition of your underwear doesn't concern me right now. I'll buy you some more."

"You could just untie my legs, and I'll take them off." I presented my best attempt at a sexy smile.

"You could have taken them off, and then I wouldn't be doing this."

I invoked my best eyelash flutters. Our gazes

Anna Hague

connected as first one knee and then the other lowered to the floor. We never lost eye contact, but his visage remained unaffected with my ploy, and I realized my seduction game needed work.

The cold steel of the blade against my skin made me squeal as he snipped the silky fabric at my thigh. First one then the—

"Owww." I jumped as much as a half-bound body could. "You cut me!"

Jordan's eyes widened as he inspected my left thigh. "Sorry. Just a little nip. It's not even blee…Oh, okay. It's just bleeding a tiny bit."

I managed to glance at the small spot of blood pooling on my thigh. "Are you sure you've done this before?"

He closed his eyes and shook his head. "I'm beginning to wonder." Jordan stood, brushing his hair from his forehead. "Are you okay? We can stop if not."

So far, I was okay, bleeding, but okay. "Yeah. I'm all right."

"All right. Good." His lips touched where he cut me, and the saltiness of his tongue on the wound made me gasp, but the sensation bore a resemblance to licking chocolate ice cream from a spoon. Involuntarily my legs wanted to flail, but the ropes held fast. The immobility intensified my awareness of helplessness, nullifying the ice cream experience.

He shifted to kiss my forehead then corralled my fidgeting right hand from my lap and positioned my whole arm parallel to the side of the chair back. He again began wrapping the silky rope around my upper arm. He made three passes before securing the knot and sliding down about three inches repeating the knots at my elbow and then my wrist. With each twist of the rope, my mercury of apprehension inched higher. Once he finished, he repeated the actions to my left arm, fastening the rope what I considered was way too tight, but I could have been overreacting, since this was my first time at the bondage thing.

I did every mind trick to slow my rapid breathing, but I was getting scared. Passing out would likely ruin the adventure for both of us. Both arms and legs struggled to accept the tethers. Only my torso and my butt had options, but Jordan ended the scant freedom by wrapping my waist and securing me to the rail on the back of the chair. Now, complete immobility fired my alarm button to high, and I couldn't stop swallowing and straining against the ropes, and so far, this arousal thing didn't even register on my pussy radar.

My anxiety grew like the mercury on a thermometer in Death Valley. Talking would help. "So now what do we do?" I was all light-hearted as if being strapped naked to a chair was an everyday thing. Didn't bother me at all.

Oh, but it did.

I never had a run in with claustrophobia, but not being able to move was fucking with my head.

"Be quiet and focus." He was serious, but not angry.

"Focus on what? I can't exactly read a book. You could turn on the TV or radio. Oh God. Please scratch my nose. It's itching." I shook my head trying to alleviate the itch. "Jordan, please scratch my nose."

"Your nose doesn't itch." He tapped his forehead. "It's all in your head. I'm going to give you something to help you concentrate."

Oh, crap. Was he going to drug me? We did not discuss drugs. My fear was short-lived as he placed a blindfold over my head. Blindfolded beat drugs, but I didn't revel in the sightless realm either.

"Jordan?"

"Shhh." He put his fingers on my lips. "Quiet."

"Can't we at least have some music?" I mumbled through closed lips. The prolonged silence suggested music was not on the to-do list.

Okay. I'd be quiet. Quiet was often a problem for me Jordan learned early in our relationship. I guess this was some sort of lesson. He told me I had a patience problem as well. I hated learning lessons because learning lessons meant either you screwed up or something bad happened.

I twisted my head in circles, as if the motion would soothe me. Right now, I had an itch problem on my nose—not in my head.

A heavy hand on my scalp put an end to the circles. "Stop."

The complete quiet in the room unnerved me. I couldn't move. I couldn't see, and the anxiety was not only returning, but also growing. I didn't know where Jordan was. After he contained my head, his scent, heat, and presence all disappeared. Was he still in the room? In the kitchen? Had he left me alone in the condo? What if he had left me? What if something bad happened and I died like this. I didn't want to die and the president of the HOA finds my skeleton still tied to a chair.

Shit…Shit…Shit. My heart pounded through my chest, and I couldn't catch my breath. Someone had placed a non-existent plastic bag over my head, and with each breath, I sucked in more imaginary plastic. "Jordan! Jordan! I can't do this! I can't do this!" Clearly, I was not Wonder Woman...the ropes held tight.

Ocean, the sun, and nearness arrived to save me. Obviously, he never left. I could smell his body—feel his heat next to me. A sweet, summery breath tickled my ear, and he was caressing my cheek. "It's all right, Baby. I'm here. Right here on my knees next to you."

The ropes didn't get any looser, and I started to cry. "I can't. I can't do this. I'm afraid."

"All right. Okay. You're fine." The blindfold still swathed my world in darkness. But he rubbed both cheeks now, and the scratch of his calloused finger grew familiar and tranquilizing.

"Listen to my voice and breathe."

His voice. Jordan's voice, so composed, so comforting, like a fleece blanket of love.

"Why are we doing this?" he asked.

"To teach me things," I managed to get out between sob hiccups.

"What else?"

"Because I said I would."

"Wasn't what I was going for, but what else?" He kissed my itchy nose.

"For your pleasure."

"And?"

"Mine?" Yeah. I wasn't getting the pleasure part yet. In fact, so far, only one of the four was working for me. I'm not sure how much pleasure a man gets out of a sobbing wife, and the single thing I was learning was I didn't think bondage was for me.

"What do we have to have in order for this to

97

work?" This was turning into a first grade rule session. We'd already established I had trouble being told what to do.

In the darkness, my mind thrashed in deep water trying to get to an unknown shore. "Trust?"

"Yes. Trust. Trust me in what way?"

Both the answer and the truth spilled from my quivering lips. "Trust you'd never hurt me?"

"Are you hurt?"

"No, but I'm un…"

"Uncomfortable?"

"Yes, and scared."

"Scared of what?" he whispered and placed a reassuring hand on my knee.

"Scared. I don't know. I don't know. I just know I'm afraid."

In my complete darkness, Jordan's voice was my radiating light. "I understand. You're scared of a few things. Not knowing what I'm doing to you, afraid it'll hurt, and most of all I think you're afraid you'll like the feeling. Angel, I'd die before I ever hurt you."

His lips brushed mine. "Do you still want to stop? We can. Your decision."

I shook my head. His declaration took away my voice.

"I need to hear your words." He squeezed my knee in encouragement.

"No. I don't want you to stop."

Because I couldn't see, my other senses sprang alive. Jordan's scent invaded my nose like a cocaine high. I imagined the sound of his heart beating in a slow steady cadence. Steady, strong, and mine.

"Angel. I want to tell you something. All of my

life, I've had this fantasy of a woman. What she looked like. What she smelled like. How the tiny hairs on her skin tickled my arms. I dreamed about the things I wanted to show her and she would allow me the honor of claiming her precious body. I dreamed of this woman for years."

His lips caressed my ear. "She's you, Angel. My fantasy is real. She's you."

Holy fuck. I think I just came with his words. I glanced at my lap to see if the chair was wet. Nothing but silky darkness. I had forgotten about the blindfold. My darkness delivered my center.

The air between us cooled. He'd left again, but then the top of my foot burned with hot breath. If I hadn't shaved my legs in anticipation of this moment, then those hairs would be standing on end.

"Focus," he whispered.

Focus, my ass. Of course. How does anyone focus when the man you love just told you you're his ultimate fantasy? I needed to send a text to Sabrina. Where was Suri when you needed her?

When his lips touched my ankle, I bucked in my bonds, convinced his fiery touch branded my leg. Each kiss landing from my calf, to my knee, dug a river of fast moving erotic fervency straight to my core.

But he stopped.

I kind of liked this part of bondage and moaned my displeasure at his pause.

"Patience, Angel," he whispered. When his lips met my inner thigh, I closed my eyes behind the blindfold, imagining his dark head between my legs. I wanted more than anything to free my hands and grab his glossy hair.

I don't know why, but I struggled under the ropes, knowing I couldn't, but wanting to free my arms. The sensation of helplessness escalated my arousal—my senses, fighting one another for top billing. With each smack of a kiss, his lips injected a burning elixir through my veins and intoxicated my blood with lusty hunger as rushes of need flowed to my core. I detected a faint essence of perspiration mixed with his scent.

I smiled to myself. He was nervous, too.

He switched from kissing to licking at a turtle's pace to my most treasured spot.

Jordan continued his assault on my thigh. My tender flesh erupted in spasms from the electrical current he was sending through my skin. I made futile attempts to rescue my leg away from his mouth. The ridiculous notion my body could physically explode with ecstasy seemed so real.

His fingers dug into my thighs with both hands, kissing, massaging, and licking. Just when I knew my rocket was about to launch, Jordan stopped. He may have stopped to let me catch my breath, and my teeth chattered as I struggled for a deep ragged gasp of oxygen.

Break over. His sweet torture between my legs with a cosmically magical tongue ensued.

The restriction of my bonds intensified my body's reaction to his slippery dance inside of me. Within minutes, I was so ready to come. My bondage virginity cherry pop was just a matter of a few more licks and sucks.

"Jordan, please, I can't wait." My whole body chilled, fevered, and trembled. My nails dug into my clenched fists, and the pain worsened my arousal.

He stopped just long enough to say "No. I want you to wait. Hold on. You'll see what happens."

"I can't," I said trying to catch my breath.

"Yes, you can. Your brain is stronger. Use your brain."

My brain. What the hell did my brain have to do with this? Okay. Think of something else. Flowers, puppies, pizza. Yes, pizza. Hot, thick, dripping with... Shit that just made things worse. Okay, Lori Mays. How much I hated Lori Mays. Lazy, dumb, sleeping with the boss. *Yep, this is working.*

"Angel. Are ya with me here? The muffled voice drifted from below.

"Jordan, what the fuck do you want?" I protested with panting breaths. "Either you're gonna let me come, or you're gonna make me think of stupid shit so I won't come. Make up your damn mind."

He stopped and started to laugh. "God, you're priceless, Angel. You're fucking hot and priceless. We'll talk about concentration another time. You win. Just let go whenever you need to, Baby."

A Nano second after his mouth resumed working the party broke out. Minstrels of orgasm traveled all the way down to the tips of my toes, and I couldn't stop the tremors. I broke out in a sweat as if I just ran a three-mile race. If the ropes weren't holding me to the chair, I would have fallen to the floor.

Jordan patted my thigh as he stood and moved far enough away the only sound I could discern was paper unwrapping. I was on birth control so we didn't need condoms. What was he doing? Then the warmth and scent of his nearby face caught my attention. He pressed his lips to mine, his tongue prying them apart.

He smelled like heavenly confection and gently forced a square chunk of dark chocolate from his mouth to mine. I swiped my tongue over and over on the velvety confection as he released my bonds. I think my skin exhaled with each loosening strand of rope, and my arms hung heavy from my shoulders. Despite the unimaginable overwhelming sex Jordan and I shared before, being bound to a wooden chair handed me the most seismic orgasm to date.

Lastly, he ended my darkness. A cool rush of air tickled my face, and I blinked several times to adjust to now being able to see. Jordan had closed the blinds to help darken the room from the midafternoon sun. He pulled me into a strong embrace, and I rested listening to his rapid heartbeat with the knowledge I had the most amazing husband ever.

"Are you okay," he asked.

I answered. "Better than okay, but I'm exhausted."

"Well then, let's take a nap." He picked me up and carried me to our bed. He had already pulled back the sheets and comforter, and as if I weighed nothing, laid me in the middle of the bed before joining me. He began massaging my arm, rubbing from shoulder to fingertip before moving on down to my leg where he repeated the process. When he had finished both arms and legs, I was in nirvana. "Is there an extra charge for this?" My eyes fluttered battling the need to sleep.

Jordan slipped his arm under my shoulders, and I instinctively snuggled on his chest. Within moments, I was asleep.

When I awoke, I didn't know if I slept a few minutes or few hours, but my husband's heating pad arms still encompassed me. He was awake, watching me with heavy lids and smoky eyes.

"What time is it?" I asked.

"It's after seven," he replied.

"Wow. I really slept."

"Little bit." He brushed a dark tendril of hair off my cheek. "We need to talk some more."

I let out a heavy sigh. "You like this talking thing, don't you? Can't we just enjoy this?"

"We are. I want to talk about how you feel now and when you sat tied in the chair. I need to know, Angel."

"In order or in general?"

His ice blue eyes sparkled with light. "However you wish."

I forced myself away from his embrace, sitting up to face him.

One of the few times I prepared what I would say before I spoke, my mind flashbacked to the scene I feared so much at first. Never in my life did I think I would willingly allow someone to tie me to a chair. I wasn't sure how I perceived this phenomenon.

"Well, clearly at first I was having trouble. Not being able to move terrified me. I wanted to stop, but when you started talking to me, the sound of your voice had this amazing effect on me. I trusted you totally. To trust you knew what you were doing, but most of all to trust you would stop if I asked. That made all of the difference."

Jordan's lips brushed my forehead. "I'm glad."

"I can't comprehend the "use your brain" comment. I tried not to think about what you were doing, and then you yelled at me to come back."

He raised his eyebrows. "Yelled at you?"

"Well, instructed might be a better word, meant the same thing at the time."

"What I was trying to do was connect your mind and body to embrace a better experience. I didn't communicate very well. I should have said to relax your brain. You were thinking too much. I wanted you to try to control your orgasm to make a stronger one. Think about your body, not everything else."

Those sexy eyes and five o'clock shadow were killing me. I was exhausted, but I wanted to go to the chair again. "I'm kinda starting to understand how not being able to do something, makes doing it so much better, like moving. Is this what attracted you to being into BDSM?"

He pondered my question for a moment. "Yes, but that's what drove me away too. I like the feeling of having power to bring someone to such a crazy level of arousal, but what I wanted and what a lot of others wanted wasn't the same thing."

"Hmm, well, I'll admit, I don't like the initial feeling of restriction, but when you start touching me, Oh my God. I was insane."

Soothing fingers touched my cheek. "I won't always do it that way."

"What do you mean?" An uncomfortable feeling was starting to creep into my chest.

"I mean, maybe at some point I won't have to touch you to give to an orgasm."

"Why would you not touch me? I'm not sure I'm in favor of your idea."

"Patience and control are the lessons." Then he winked at me. "And sometimes it's just all about fuckin with ya."

"How come you can say 'fuck' and I can't?"

He pulled me over until I was on my back. "Because I make the rules."

God, I loved this man.

Chapter Seven

I don't know if Jessica was wide-eyed because I told her about my first BDSM session or just about the whole story in general. She was failing miserably at trying to keep an indifferent face. I put myself in her place. I suppose I might feel the same way, but then again, Jessica was a reporter getting a story, and she's the one who put out the feelers. What did she think she would get? Couples who only ate peanut butter?

Again, I waited until she caught up with her notes. She would go back, read something again, as if writing a grocery list. Occasionally, she would nod, purse her lips, or flinch as if she had an idea.

What surprised me, the more I talked, the more aroused I was getting.

Cathartic.

I loved my life now. I loved my husband. He gave me a freedom to feel without guilt. At some point, I would explain. Before this life, I coped with my sexuality, but being bound freed me to embrace my needs. When I stepped across the threshold to this life, I found my true self. I was Alice and my new Wonderland extracted so many emotions from euphoria to devastation to re-discovery.

"Alrighty," she said after a huge exhale of air. "So the weekend went fairly well, you're saying. So what about…did anything change when you went back to work?"

"Work did change. Some things became an issue."

****

Monday morning, I walked through the doors of Millennial Publishing smiling. You know the confidence you have when you just got laid? Well, there I was striding into the office like I owned the damned place—until I stepped into my cubicle to find the bane of my existence sitting on my desk holding the framed photo of Jordan and I.

Lori Fucking Mays.

"Did you buy this frame and photoshop yourself into the picture already installed?" the viperous bitch said.

"He's my husband. I'm sure you read the e-mail I sent out to everyone stating I recently got married," I replied.

Throughout my life, some people pissed me of, but I never hated anyone in my life, but I hated her. She was lazy, always pawning her work off on everyone—me. The only reason she retained a job had everything to do with her propensity for sucking Mr. Johnson's Johnson, our president and CEO.

She continued to ogle my husband's photo while uncrossing her long luxurious legs and opening her thighs. "I saw the e-mail. I just have a hard time believing the guy in the photo is the guy you married. I mean, really. I'm look'n at him. Look'n at you."

I walked over and snatched the photo from her hands. How dare she spread her legs on my desk and have photo sex with my husband. "What do you want, Lori?"

What I hated most about her was me. I let her get

under my skin. "I've got work to do."

"Well,"—she stood stretching like a cat—"I sent you Tyson Clammer's manuscript to look over. I'm really pretty busy,"

Busy sucking dick.

"If you could just go over the pages and give me your notes…"

"I'm not doing your job anymore. You can't even do your job. I'd be willing to bet you can't even tell the difference between 'there, their, and they're.' "

She straightened when my invisible knife struck her. "Don't flatter yourself. You think you're better than me? Look who keeps getting promoted."

"That's because I can't open my mouth as wide as you can."

Her skin flushed red, while her eyes bulged. "I need it back by Thursday." She huffed away. Lori Mays would one day be my downfall.

The one thing our clash did do for me was to take my mind off being self-conscious about the scarf tied so expertly around my neck by my husband. I turned on my computer and began to work, ignoring the email attachment from LMays.

Chapter Eight

Just weeks into our marriage, I had a public coming out of sorts. The Circle City Association for Business sponsored a charity ball and fundraiser. Fairland Entertainment was a major contributor and CEO Bernhard Levendar served on the board. His golden boy, Jordan, headed the planning committee for the ball. So my guess was he would be spending little time with me at the ball, but because few in his company knew me and even fewer attended our wedding, I would be playing the role of circus pony on lunge line for the evening.

I stood in front of the full-length mirror in our bedroom, smoothing the wispy, flowing fire engine red dress we purchased. The hem touched the floor, forcing me to wear the "fuck me" silver strappy pumps I loved. The name rang true because every time I wore them, Jordan couldn't keep his hands off me, and at times, he wanted me to wear them during our scenes, but more often than not, the hooker boots had a higher return rate for investment.

"I just want to rip the thing off and fuck you right here on the floor, all while I watch in the mirror," he said while chewing my neck just enough I feared him leaving a mark for everyone to see.

"I wouldn't be thrilled. You know, exhibitionism not really my thing."

Jordan had removed my collar before I showered, and now he set a black box on the bed.

"What's in the box?"

He opened the lid to the box exposing its contents.

When I peered inside, my jaw dropped. Sitting a black velvet bed was a silver cuff necklace. About an inch wide, the front sported black filigree design almost Celtic in nature.

I touched the cool silver. "Oh, Jordan it's beautiful."

He place the cuff around my neck, and I held my breath as the chill of the silver metal touching my skin expanded to other parts of my body. Although looser than my collar, the weight of the metal made me very aware of what I was wearing. After weeks of wearing the leather collar, I became accustomed to the feel and almost unaware of the band signifying my connection to my husband, but the beautiful piece of jewelry surrounding my neck, made me very conscientious of my choice.

"You don't think people will notice, do you?" I fingered the smooth silver.

He whisper kissed the back of my neck sending chills up and down my spine. "I think they'll notice how stunning my wife is, and wonder how did this guy get that girl."

His hand slipped into my dress caressing my breast and giving my nipple a pinch. So focused on the feel of the cuff, I flinched at his touch at the sharp pain. I slapped away his hand.

"I think we should go before we end up putting some nasty wrinkles in these fine clothes. If I spend too much time gawking at you in your suit, my hand's gonna be hot on your zipper."

I meant every word. With my favorite black suit hugging his broad shoulders and narrow waist. *Oh my God.* Then add the white shirt and light blue tie—a perfect complement to the ice blue of his eyes. My husband was a huge bowl of eye candy, and I alone had permission to indulge.

He pinched my nipple again. "I'm thinking our next session should include nipple clamps."

I shuddered. Something about the words 'nipple' and 'clamp' didn't go together in my vocabulary or my fantasies.

I broke from his grasp and faced him. "We should go and see this spectacular ball you've planned." *Nice way to change the subject.*

"It wasn't just me. A lot of people worked very hard." He tipped my chin. "I know I said this once before, but as a reminder, there is one person who will be there tonight who I don't want you talking to. Just walk away from him."

I sighed. Jordan had said this way more than once before. He decreed I was not to speak to Cameron Terry. I don't know why. Jordan wasn't forthcoming with why he didn't like this guy, but he was so adamant about me staying away from him, I wondered if this guy was some sort of serial killer. "Yes, I know. Stay away from Cameron Terry. The only problem is I don't know what he looks like. So how can I stay away from someone I'm clueless about?"

Still holding my chin, he said. "I'll point him out when we get there."

"Maybe he won't be there."

"He'll be there."

****

When we arrived at the Indiana Ballroom, my jaw dropped at the scene. The historic hall resembled a European village complete with plaster columns, stucco facades, doors, balconies, and stairways. The roof resembled a night sky with stars twinkling down from overhead. The planning committee accented the already quaint and elegant setting with Italian style fountains and two gondolas sitting at opposite ends of the room. Ornate candelabras decorated with grapevines and flowers adorned each table. Servers in tuxedos carried bottles of Italian wine and trays of meats and cheeses. The A Night in Venice theme promised a romantic evening.

"Jordan, this place looks…"

Before I could finish, a young woman grabbed Jordan's arm. "Mr. Caldera, we have a big problem."

She kept pulling him away from me. "Julie, Julie. Calm down. I'll take care of it. Just show me," he said to the frantic associate.

He released my hand from his. "Angel. This won't take but a few minutes. I'll be right back."

"Sure. I'll just admire your work."

Jordan left, and I strolled about the room marveling at the beauty of the place. More than a few minutes passed and no Jordan, so I sat on a bench next to one of the fountains. I left my phone at home so I wouldn't be tempted to check the screen all night. Without my phone, all I could do was to check out the crowd.

"May I join you?" The deep masculine voice startled me. At first, a nicely manicured hand offered me a glass of white wine. When I followed the hand to the face attached to the voice, my heart skipped a betraying beat. Damn, he was handsome. With amber-colored hair and a day's scruff, the man with deep green eyes stared through me, and my nipples betrayed me.

"Sure." Without hesitation, I accepted the wine and scooted to the edge to make room for an alluring stranger.

"Exquisite here tonight isn't it?" He sipped his wine and nodded to me, prompting me to drink as well.

"Yes. They did a fantastic job of decorating. My husband worked very hard. I hope everyone has a nice time."

His gaze bore through me, forcing me to turn my attention away from him. I recovered enough to take a drink of the wine.

"Your husband. And who might he be?"

"Jordan Caldera."

He nodded, but something about his demeanor told me Jordan and him were acquainted. "Ohhh yeah. Well Mr. Caldera is very good at what he does."

He inched ever so subtly closer to me. I didn't really mind too much. He smelled fabulous, too. Not like Jordan, but different…woodsier.

I swirled the wine in my glass trying not to look at this very attractive man. Was he eliciting some weird pheromone to draw me closer? "I'm sorry. I didn't catch your name."

Mr. Attractive extended his hand. "Cameron Terry."

Shit.

Chapter Nine

Cameron Terry held my hand longer than socially appropriate, and I hated myself a little for enjoying the attention. "Oh. Well. I'm Emma Caldera."

He released my hand, but a little guilt lingered in me.

"Your picture doesn't do you justice."

"My picture?"

"Jordan has a photo of the two of you on his desk. You are much more beautiful in person."

I flushed. "Well. Thank you. I think the dress is very forgiving."

"I don't think it's the dress. I think you're flattering the dress. Jordan hasn't said a lot about you, though. What do you do besides being beautiful?"

In one gulp, I finished the wine. I should have left. Leaving would have been the best decision, but he was just a harmless flirt. I should know, I'd played the game for years. Why Jordan hated him, I don't know. "I work at a publishing company as a low level copy editor. Somewhat boring. What do you do at Fairland?"

He crossed his legs and sat straighter. "Jordan didn't mention me?"

"Briefly. He didn't go into any details." *Other than to stay away. Nope, he said nothing about you being both hot and charming.*

"He doesn't talk about work much. We do other

things." *Yes. Yes, we do kinky things. I bet you'd like to know.*

Excellent. Judging from the non-reaction, I was certain I didn't say the words aloud.

He handed me a business card. *Cameron Terry, Director of Public Relations.*

In addition to the basic work e-mail and phone number, his personal cell number also graced the card. "What's this for?"

"If you need something or have a problem and Jordan's not around, just call me. I'd be happy to help."

I stared at the card, not sure what he meant by the statement. I supposed he was being friendly, and other than being a grade A flirt, he was harmless. Still though, if Jordan spied the card, he'd go ballistic. "I don't know if it's a good idea."

"It's just a business card, for an emergency. That's all. I'm not the monster your husband believes I am." He winked.

I rammed the card in the tiny purse and scanned the area to make sure no one witnessed my clandestine act. Time to find more wine.

Staring through the empty glass, I discerned a distorted image of Jordan approaching us. When I looked around the glass, I was wrong. The distorted features I believed I imagined were real.

He was pissed.

Cameron stood as Jordan converged upon us. "Caldera."

"Terry." He said through gritted teeth.

"I was just getting to know your beautiful wife." He leaned into Jordan's personal space. "You know, you shouldn't leave a woman as enchanting as Emma alone."

At the use of my name, Jordan's neck reddened. "If you'll excuse us. We have people to mingle with."

He extended his hand, and I had no choice but to accept. He clamped my hand to his and pulled me from the bench to his side without a pause. As we walked away, Cameron called, "Till next time."

I kept stumbling trying to match Jordan's frenzied pace. "Slow the fuck down, will ya?" I kept from screaming even though I'm sure my voice was less than pleasant.

He found a small private alcove and backed me up against the wall. He braced his arm above my head and not with the intent to kiss me. "One thing. I asked you to do, one thing. Stay away from Cameron Terry, and I'm gone five minutes, and you're practically in his lap."

Practically in his lap. Are you kidding me?

Wow. I was the only rational one in attendance. In direct contrast to the simmering blood gathering for a war, I crossed my arms in slow motion across my chest and smiled into his icy gaze. "Let me make a point of information…Mr. Caldera. I asked you what Cameron looked like." I poked my finger in his chest. "You said you would show me when we arrived." I poked again. "You ran off as soon as we arrived to put out some fire only the *Great One* could handle." I kept poking, finding a sweet spot causing him to wince. "I sat by myself, not speaking to anyone waiting for you, and I quote, 'just a few minutes,' to end. He came up to me. I didn't know who he was. If *someone* had given me some clues, I might have been able to avoid the situation." I shoved him away and stepped from his towering frame. "You won't even tell me why you don't like him. So this whole scenario is ridiculous."

I crossed my arms again and leaned into the wall waiting for his response. Right now, I relished watching him squirm, struggling to find the words to admit his error.

"Thank you for pointing out my mistake. I shouldn't have deserted you." He ran his hand through his hair, but the locks sprang into their perfect original location. "When I saw you sitting there talking with that asshole, I lost my mind. I'm sorry. I don't like him."

"Well, then fire him."

Jordan sighed. "I can't. He doesn't work in my department, and even if he did, I can't fire someone for personal reasons. Also, he's damn good at his job."

I edged closer to my husband and rested my hand on his shoulder. He tensed under my touch. "He's very charming."

"Yes he is." Jordan stiffened.

"He's very attractive."

He stared at the wall. "I suppose, but I don't know how to judge what constitutes attractiveness in a man."

I stood on the tips of my toes and feathered my lips to Jordan's ear. "But you know what he's not?"

"What." He sighed.

How could a man so confident and large look so vulnerable? "He's not you. Only you can make me feel such joy I want to scream. Sometimes I do scream. Sometimes at work, I think about what you do to me, and my panties get so wet, I'm embarrassed."

Jordan grabbed my waist and rammed my body against the wall. He attacked me, holding my head hostage, while his lips assaulted and ravaged my mouth.

My legs couldn't hold me. I slumped down the wall despite the stucco scraping my bare back. This time, scratches would decorate me. He wrapped an arm around my waist, holding me, keeping me from falling.

"I wish we could go home," he said, nibbling my ear.

"Just use this time to plan how you are going to make me scream later."

"God Damn, I want to leave."

Chapter Ten

"So did you go home?" Jessica laughed as she chewed on her pen.

"After a round of glad handing, and later I did a lot of screaming." *Till my throat was raw.*

A sense of pride hit me knowing how far I had come from the woman who was so tongue-tied she had trouble speaking to the man she would marry and who had tied her to a chair or pole and fucked her senseless.

I was a different person.

"Before we go any further, I would like to talk a little about how being in my relationship is, how I feel inside, how this has changed me. I get how most people can't understand this feeling I have being a submissive to my husband."

Jessica gave me an enthusiastic smile. "Great. Sure, people wouldn't be able to understand unless they at least know your feelings, whether they can relate to those feelings or not. This is so weird to me, but some might appreciate the enlightenment. I'm just fascinated. Am I rambling? I'm sorry if I am."

I know I wasn't much older than this reporter was, but somehow, she acted like such a kid. Did I really want her writing about my life? No big deal because no one would ever know who I am.

"When I'm with my husband, I feel this intense longing that has little to do with BDSM, and at the same time everything to do with it. The first moment when I see him, whether in the morning when I wake or when I see him after work, or when I walk in a restaurant to meet him for lunch, and he stands up to wait for me, time stands still, and all I see and all I know is him. There is no ticking of time, no high or low tide, or full or quarter moon. It is only us. Surreal may be the best word. I know we're both there, but what I'm seeing is all blurry, except my husband. It's like being in a bubble in the center of frozen time, and when he touches me, the blur explodes and the pieces disintegrate, and in my mind, we're the only two people in the world."

"You're giving me chills." Jessica put her pen in her mouth to chew the tip.

"When I'm bound to the bed or chair or something else. When there is no possible way I can escape anything he's about to do, resignation, realization, is a gift I give to my husband and is a gift to myself. There's no freer feeling than when your soul soars."

Jessica's fingers flew over the keyboard trying to get every word. When she stopped, she reached for the water bottle, downed a big gulp, and blew out a breath.

"So did you ever find out why your husband hated this guy?"

"I did, a few weeks later."

****

When Jordan came home from work Friday evening, his attention span measured like a gnat, until after we played a little "tie me up and let's insert chocolate in a few select places." Once I'd showered and climbed into bed to snuggle with him, he did seem ready to talk.

"You're getting used to and enjoy what we're doing, yes?" He smoothed my hair as I lay across his chest with my ear to his heart.

"I do. Sometimes I'm a little overwhelmed, but I know I can trust you."

He kept fidgeting with my hair, lacing the strands between his fingers and pulling through the ends. "I want to introduce you to some of the people in the group I used to belong to."

"The kinky group?" *Did I want to meet these people?*

I couldn't see his face, but I'm pretty sure he did an eye roll. "Yes, the kinky group. There's a party tomorrow night, and I would like to go and have you meet some people."

I raised my head for a second. "So what goes on at these parties?"

"A lot is just like any other party. You know, food, drink, conversation. When I say drinks, though, I mean no alcohol. Not allowed."

"What? How much fun can a sober party be?"

He gathered a fist full of my hair and tugged, forcing me to face him. "Alcohol interferes with your ability to be clear-headed, and if you are in scene, then you need all of your senses sharp."

"Are these like orgies?"

He banged his head against the headboard. "You're testing me aren't you? There are opportunities to meet and play with other people." He tugged my hair again. I rather liked the motion of forcing me to face him. "You won't be doing that. Also, usually there is a demonstration of some sort of kink."

"And we all watch?" Up close and personal. Wow.

"If you want." He shifted his body, moving my hip from his balls. Penises and balls are funny things. One minute they're take no prisoners and the next they're whining about being crushed.

"Are most people into kink exhibitionists? Because I'm not into showing the world my shit." That's not only a "no," but a "hell no."

"Ahhh." He scrutinized the crack in the ceiling while his feet fidgeted. "Not everyone, but yeah, sure, some are."

"Are you?"

I could feel his body shift his weight from side to side. "I'm not opposed, but you're not comfortable I see."

"I'm not comfortable with it." End of story. I hated trying on jeans and bathing suits. No way in hell would I let people watch me naked *and* watch me have an orgasm.

"Would you object to watching a demo?"

Would I balk at watching a demo? In my mind, I equated demo with watching a porn flick, only live. I'd watched porn a few times. Didn't make me want to claw my eyes out. So, I guessed I could watch. "I suppose."

"Well, then I say we go to a party tomorrow." He rolled me over on my back and planted his body on top of mine, suppressing my breathing in a most delightful way. His forehead touched mine, and my heart melted.

****

"So, what do you wear to a sex orgy?" I yelled from the bedroom into the bathroom while Jordan showered.

The squeak of the shower faucets turning informed

me he was finished, so I walked to the space between the bedroom and bathroom in time to catch the show as he stepped from the shower, dripping all over the mat and floor. I swallowed hard. Life is just not fair for someone to be all wet and hot at the same time.

"Something sexy." He responded wiping his legs with a towel. "And stop saying orgy."

I rummaged through the drawer and found my black satin and lace corset we'd purchased online. Trimmed in red ribbon, the corset had silver stays and red lacings. When Jordan laced me up, my boobs bordered on awesome.

"No." Jordan's glare focused on the item dangling in my hand.

"You said something sexy. This is the best I got. You cut up all my underwear if you so remember."

He yanked the corset from my hand. "This." He hung the thing in my face. "Is for my eyes only."

So, I sat on the edge of the bed naked, crossing my legs and my arms. "Well, then. You find me something *sexy*, but falls under the category not *for your eyes only*."

By the time we left, Jordan had outfitted me in a black mini skirt, black leather tank top, no underwear, and my hooker boots. I wrapped a thin black-silk scarf around my collar for cover until we arrived at the party. I told Jordan not to leave me standing alone on the sidewalk because I was convinced someone would come by and offer me twenty bucks for a quickie.

"Twenty bucks?" A possessive hand to the small of my back, guided me out of the door. "I'd pay way more than twenty."

He drove to the far west side of suburban

Indianapolis, not far from where Jordan's parents lived. He pulled into the driveway of a tri-level partial brick home with a huge detached three-car garage.

"Nice place for a party." I turned to Jordan. "Who lives here?"

"Mark and his wife Laura. They host a great deal of the parties because they have so much space. Seven bedrooms, rec room, basement. Pool. Lots of places to have fun." He raised his eyebrows in a hopeful manner.

I frowned. "Can I at least be in the door five minutes before you try to fuck me in a strange bed like I'm at a frat party?"

He checked his watch. "Five minutes. Hell, I'd thought it'd take longer."

I stuck out my tongue.

He smiled, followed however by and a serious turn in his demeanor. "When we go in, you need to be a little more…"

"More what? I'm already like borderline hooker here."

"That's what I mean. You need to be more subdued."

I waved my hand to showcase my sexy slutty outfit.

"As in?" What could he be talking about? As a general rule, I wasn't the girl dancing on the table at parties. I could *at* times have a smart mouth, but I doubt I would enlighten people I didn't know.

He squeezed my hand hard enough to get my attention. "Remember when I told you about protocol?"

"Yes. Things you said you weren't really into, but I've a feeling we're about to get into."

"You're collar signifies to other men you're mine,

and it's understood any contact with them has to go through me."

"You mean if they want to fuck me, they have to ask you? Do I get a say in this?" *I really can't help myself sometimes.*

"Owww." He squeezed my hand so hard I expected to find a bent finger.

"God Dammit Angel. Would you just listen and refrain from commentary for thirty seconds?

My knuckles stung from the rap with the imaginary ruler.

"I'll just make this easy. Two rules. Just stay with me and don't initiate conversation unless it's with another sub."

He pulled my hand to his mouth. kissing the spot where just moments before, the hard knock of a ruler landed.

"And this is supposed to be fun?" A root canal analogy crossed my mind

"And educational."

As soon as we walked through the door of the massive home, I had no qualms about sticking next to Jordan and keeping my mouth shut. I estimated about fifty strangers in attendance. Instinctively, I affixed myself to my husband as we made our way through the foyer to the kitchen where he found who I assumed to be our host.

A sandy-haired man, almost as tall as Jordan, but more broad, turned and a huge smile swept across his face. He grabbed Jordan's hand in a vigorous handshake before embracing him.

"Mr. Caldera. I can't believe you're here. Wow, it's been too long, buddy."

He turned his attention to me, but I remained silent.

"And who is this lovely lady?

Jordan wrapped his arms across my shoulders and kissed the top of my head. "This is my wife, Emma. Emma, this is Mr. Conners."

Still unsure of what to do, I smiled and nodded— thought about curtsying. I almost buckled from a nudge in the back of my knee. *Permission to speak granted? Asshole.*

"Hello." I didn't know what else to say. *You have the perfect home for sex parties?*

I assumed Mr. Conners sensed my unease because he glanced around the vast kitchen. "Laura is here somewhere. She went to the pantry for more chips, I think." His eyes brightened. "Oh, there she is. Laura come here and see who just walked in."

I followed his gaze to see a statuesque redheaded goddess with porcelain skin and green eyes. She wore an emerald green corset, a black leather mini skirt, and her collar was a braided gold choker with a filigree heart in the center. When she joined us, Laura lowered her gaze and waited.

Protocol.

"Laura," Mark said. "Mr. Caldera is back, and he's brought his wife Emma."

I could see a flash of surprise as she briefly raised her eyes.

"Welcome, Emma. So nice to meet you." She extended her hand in a genuine greeting.

"Why don't you show Emma around, while we catch up," Mark kissed her cheek in dismissal.

Laura grasped my hand to lead me away from the safety of my husband into a den of iniquity with an amazon queen. My hand slipped from hers, but she gripped again and toppled my resistance.

"I'm sorry. My hands get sweaty when I'm nervous."

"S'okay. If this is your first party, then it's understandable."

I held on as we maneuvered through a crowd of women wearing scant little clothing and men who were dressed like they were about to watch a football game on television. I wasn't sure why their attire bothered me. The women could fit their outfits in the glove box of a smart car, and while I found nothing outright wrong with the men's attire, I concluded...I don't know, a little sexism filled the room. Jordan dressed in jeans, but they were black, and he wore a white dress shirt and black boots. We matched a little.

As Laura pointed out different areas of the house, she brushed by some of the bedrooms not stopping at the occupied rooms.

"If people are using the rooms, why don't they shut the doors," I asked her.

"Safety reasons. Behind closed doors, someone could get hurt. Not everyone here is part of a couple. They're here to play. This way, you have sort of an audience, and people are mindful of what they're doing."

It all sounded nice, but what I really wanted to know was who cleaned up the mess the next day?

We walked into their master bedroom slash penthouse suite. The large four-poster bed radiated romance with the cherry-wood furniture and white bed linens. The masculine-feel furnishings complemented the feminine touch to the throw pillows and gauzy curtains.

She opened a set of French doors to reveal a balcony overlooking the pool area.

"We haven't opened the pool yet for the summer, but when we do, you and Jordan should come over."

"Thank you. You're very nice to offer."

Laura brushed a stray hair from my face. I couldn't help but stare at the stunning woman. The warmth of her fingers radiated through my skin, and a knot of panic grew in my stomach. *Does she think I'm a switch hitter*? I don't care what turns people on, but I prefer to stick to one team.

"I know the first time coming to these parties can be a little over whelming, so if you need or you and Jordan need to get away from the commotion, feel free to come up here and relax."

Whew.

"Here, let's sit." She directed me to a wicker loveseat on the balcony.

"I'm pretty nervous. I don't know what to do or expect." I chose the end closest to the door. If I needed to get away, I'd rather run through the bedroom than jump over the balcony.

She patted my leg. "I can tell by the way Jordan held on to you how much he loves you. He wouldn't bring you anywhere he wasn't comfortable. People are here because they want to be and here they can be free to be who they are. We're a no judgement zone."

She propped her legs on the balcony railing. "How long have you and Jordan been married?"

"A few months. We had a rather short engagement. Some may have thought us getting married so fast was a bad idea, but I was sure he was everything I wanted and needed."

"Jordan is a terrific guy. We missed him when he didn't come to the parties anymore, but we understood."

"He told me why he left the life."

"Jordan isn't your stereotypical Dominant, and I think he was a little conflicted about what some subs want and what he wanted."

I'd known Laura less than twenty minutes, and already I was ready to tell her anything. "I was a little…no a lot shocked when he told me about his BDSM desires. I'd never had any experience before."

"And now?" Her eyes sparked with interest.

"And now. I think I've found the missing piece I didn't know was missing. Still though, I'm afraid to tell anyone."

"Oh, I hear ya. I'm a teacher. Can you imagine what would happen if my students' parents found out?"

She dropped her legs, stood, and leaned against the rail all in one graceful motion.

"I wasn't like you. I figured out myself in college. However, I didn't have complete fulfillment until I met Mark. Now, unlike Jordan, he's a very stereotypical Dominant. He reigns at these parties, and he reigns in the bedroom. No questions asked, and I get wet just thinking about discipline." She offered her hand to me. "Come on, demo in five minutes."

"Are you and Mark?"

"Yes, tonight we are, and if I'm late, there'll be hell to pay. Like I said, he reigns." She shivered, but a huge knowing smile spread across her face.

****

I leaned into Jordan, his arms wrapped like a vise

around my waist. Part of me was embarrassed at the scene I was witnessing, but an even bigger part—my woman part to be exact, throbbed with arousal.

Bound to a pole in the rec room, Laura answered every question her Dominant husband asked with "Yes, Sir or No, Sir." Words spoken such love and devotion were not those of a woman disrespected by her husband's commands.

I performed enough internet research to know the toys Mark had in his hand were a flogger and a crop. First, he danced the laces of the flogger across her back. Then, he snapped the leather pad of the crop against her buttocks. He intermingled each flick against her flesh, which bloomed pink from the strikes. While she flinched at each stroke, Laura's facial expression of pure bliss made my own skin blush with need.

My body texted to Jordan the intense reaction I was having to witnessing such a display. "Would you like to go upstairs?" He whispered in my ear as his lips brushed the tip.

His hand fingered the collar latched around my throat. Every smear of contact from the leather against my skin signaled the nucleus of my universe I needed his touch. I pretended to ponder his question.

"No," I whispered back. Despite my heightened need, I couldn't. I wasn't ready to have a sexual escapade in a stranger's home, while other partygoers also engaged. Hell, in college, I was the one who talked my girlfriends out of doing someone at a party. Bri's mom considered me slut, but I had standards.

Still I squirmed with every stroke to Laura's back.

"Then I'll just make you crazy right here." His husky tone caused a moment of panic. What was he going to do?

But the moment passed as Jordan stiffened, cementing me to his body. "What the hell are you doing here?"

Chapter Eleven

I turned my head to see Cameron Terry walking toward us with a casual confidence. Cameron Terry. *No shit?* The forbidden man was into kink, and here he was not two feet away.

"Mr. Caldera. Is that any way to greet someone?" His smug grin caused a compression on my waist from my husband's flexing arms. Any more and I wouldn't be able to breathe. Good thing I didn't wear the corset.

Now, my interest in the flogging of Laura vanished, and I focused on the scruffy-faced hot man who so pissed off my husband. He stood just close enough I smelled his woodsy scent.

The dark tone of my husband's voice reverberated through me. "My desk calendar said you were on vacation. I wouldn't have come had I known you were going to be here."

"Caldera, Caldera, you always had trouble coming in my presence." He winked. "It's common knowledge," he said. I sensed Jordan's blood pressure rising with the climbing heat of his body expressing through me.

"We all know your history." He kept smiling, but sarcasm prevailed in his tone.

Jordan's arms interlocked across the top of my breasts. "Why don't you just get the fuck away from us?"

He turned his focus to the demo." Maybe I want to learn something…Oh wait, I don't need any instruction. You do."

A man who resembled an ex-offensive lineman stepped between us. "Is there a problem between you? We don't need this."

Cameron held up his hands. "I've no problem."

Jordan maintained his stance. "I think we're leaving."

He unwrapped himself from me before taking my hand. Without a word, we left the house and walked to the car.

Once inside, Jordan started the car.

"Jordan, do you care to explain what your less than acceptable exchange was all about?"

"No. I do not care to explain." He shifted the car into drive but didn't release the brake.

I sighed and did the woman thing of staring out the passenger window. "For someone who strives for honesty, you're being a son of a bitch of a liar by omission. I was more than a little surprised to see Cameron Terry walk in. You never said he was into this scene, but that doesn't explain why you hate him."

He slammed the gear into Park. "All right. Remember when I told you when I couldn't give subs what they wanted, and they went to someone else?"

"Yeeeaah."

"Terry was *that* someone else."

"So, he stole your girls." I smiled at my high school reference.

"Put rather simply, yes."

My hand found its way to his silky hair and latched onto a handful, yanking his head in my direction.

"Owww!" He snapped his hand around my wrist, preventing me from pulling any more, but I refused to let go of his hair.

"What the hell is wrong with you?" I curled my fingers deeper tightening around the roots. His jaw twitched, but he remained still, even though getting me to release his hair required little of his strength. "You think because Cameron Terry comes in with some vast intimate knowledge of how to make a girl scream, I'm going to run over and fall to my knees? What the fuck, Jordan? I don't know what we're doing half the time. How am I supposed to know what he can do? Give me a little credit. I'm your wife. I love you, you dumb fuck!"

I wanted to uncurl my fingers from his hair. I really did, but his ridiculous assumption kept me hanging on.

"Are you done?" His hand tightened on my wrist.

I wasn't sure if he meant yelling or yanking. I let go and slumped against the seat. "Yes, I'm finished." I wished for the blindfold to block out everything except my desire to calm down.

Even closing my eyes failed because my brain shifted into overdrive. "Didn't we have this conversation at the gala?"

Since darkness heightens the other senses, I shivered from the grinding of his teeth pelting my ears.

"I thought you said you were finished." The leather seat squeaked with bodies shifting weight, and the slight g-force of the car lurching into Drive signaled the end of my first play party.

"I am now. We can go home."

"Thank you."

Just a few miles away from the house, curiosity got

the best of me. "So what did he do for those women, they all ran to him?"

He slammed his fist on the dash. "Angel! I'm ordering you to stop talking about Terry."

I narrowed my gaze. "You can't order me to do anything. We're not in the bedroom."

"Like you listen there, either. You wait until we get home. Think how turned on you were thirty minutes ago. I'm going to do that and more, and you're going to be hearing the Rolling Stones in your head, because you're getting no satisfaction, my dear wife. I'm goin' to string you up and pump you until you're ready to explode and then leave you begging me to end your misery."

I considered stretching my foot and smashing the accelerator.

Chapter Twelve

"Alrighty then." Jessica stopped typing and licked her lips. Her chest expanded almost as fast as her fingers hit the keyboard.

I think I just turned her on with my vignette. I waited until her breathing returned to normal. This girl could very well hyperventilate. "I told you I would be a little graphic."

"Yes, you did, and I'm glad you are. I just don't know what I was expecting, but this just may be a story readers will freak out about."

"Freak out good or freak out bad?" Either way, I was in for the long haul.

"Either way. It doesn't matter. You want your stories to evoke emotion in a reader. Emotion doesn't have to be good or bad. In the print world, emotion equals money."

That made sense. When this story was published, I'm not sure I could read my story in print, but reliving my history now made me realize how much life changed for me in such a short time.

"If you don't mind," she said, "I would like to go back to something, you said earlier. You said only one other person knew about your life, but by accident. Would you tell me about how the person found out? I mean, choosing this life is one thing, but keeping the secret from everyone else has got to be stressful."

Stressful couldn't even begin to describe what hiding my collar was like. My best friend, Sabrina was not with me the night Jordan and I met. But since third grade, we were inseparable, and when the most important change in my life happened, I couldn't force myself to tell her.

"I have only one regret about this life. Keeping my decision from my best friend was one of the most difficult parts of my life. She and I did everything together. She kept me sane while I was freaking out about getting married, but she didn't know why I was freaking out. Her partially correct perception was I was a love-struck crazy bride."

I traveled back to some of the times I wanted to tell her but couldn't find the words to convey my confession. "Hey, just thought you'd like to know I get off now on kink."

The day she found out still haunts my heart.

****

One day, after work, I met Sabrina in the alley behind my office. Her workplace was just a few blocks away, and we were walking to Miller's Pub for a quick drink.

"I feel like you're keeping something from me. You and Jordan fine? I mean, I know you just got married and should be deliriously happy, but somehow you seem different." She stared right into my face, and I kicked a rock with each new step—anything to not look at her.

I had an answer for everything. "I'm deliriously happy. Getting married is a big deal. I mean there are lots of things you weren't expecting. Who's going to cook dinner? Who does the laundry? Things like that.

Marriage is all very new to both of us. We're very happy, though. Who wouldn't be happy with a guy like the one I have? He's amazing." All in one breath.

Sabrina's glare pierced through my eyes like a laser. She didn't buy what I was selling. "No, for real, Emma, what's up with the change in wardrobe?"

Emma. She called me Emma. A bead of sweat trickled down my spine.

"What do you mean?" As a rule, I sucked at lying, but this time I was sure my acting skills prevailed.

"Don't give me your crap." Sabrina's face wrinkled and flushed red. "Since you married Jordan, your whole style has changed. Seems all you wear are scarves and turtlenecks. Girl it's summer, and you're still wearing a scarf. Before Jordan, you had one scarf in your wardrobe. Now you have about thirty."

"You're crazy." My mind blacked out. Beads of sweat popped out on my forehead, and one trickled down my face, settling in my eye. How could I tell her now, when I couldn't tell her before.

"Yeah. I don't think so." Sabrina slapped her hands on my shoulders, which put me in panic mode. I tensed and turned away from her inquisition. "I mean this." Her hands circled around my neck. Her eyes widened. She could feel the collar.

"What the hell?" She attempted to tear away the scarf. I grabbed her hand to stop her. I panicked. She couldn't find out.

But she did. She tugged the scarf enough to expose the leather collar. Seeing my altered life shocked her hand away. "What the hell is going on, Emma?"

I closed my eyes. "I didn't want you to know. It's all good, Bri. It's not what you think."

"What I think? What I think is your husband has made you his little sex slave. What a son of a bitch. I'll shove my foot so far up his ass…"

I'd never witnessed her so angry. Sabrina and subdued were lifelong partners.

"Stop," I screamed. "It's not Jordan. It's me. I mean. Yes, he's the one who showed me. He opened up the conversation, but I said yes. I agreed." Sweat poured down my face, and my breaths were coming rapid, but I couldn't take in enough oxygen. I fought the dizziness swirling in my brain.

Sabrina stood with her mouth open. Her face paled, and I didn't recognize the woman who guarded my deepest secrets. This time I had neglected to tell her the biggest one of my life.

"Bri, I'm happy about wearing this." I tried to throw in every positive adjective I could think of in a desperate situation. I was so frantic *happy* was the best I could do.

Moisture bubbled in her eyes. "You can't be, Emma. How could anybody be? For one, you don't tell me, your best friend, and two, you're trying to justify…" She waved her finger from my head to my toes. "God, I don't know you at all. For most of our lives, I thought I knew everything about you. I naively believed I was the one who you would share everything with. Look at this. You're so ashamed you couldn't even tell me."

The tears raced down her face. How could I fix this? I had destroyed the trust of my best friend.

She made a futile attempt to wipe her cheeks. "I'm through with you, Emma. Is your name even Emma anymore, or should I call you Slave, Slut, something along those lines?"

Her words stabbed deep in my heart. She turned to distance herself from everything about me. "Sabrina, please, don't. Wait, let me explain to you."

She never turned, just flipped me the bird and disappeared around the corner of the building. My concern flipped from my disappearing friend to who else might have seen. Frenetic fingers rewrapped the scarf around my neck, but I was alone in more ways than one. This shit storm had ripped away my heart.

My ringtone cheerfully blasted from my pocket. I snatched the phone and found Jordan displayed on the screen. Like every phone call this time of day, he wanted to talk about dinner, but I couldn't talk right now and not to him. I touched my scarf. The silk fabric concealed my collar, but not me. My façade of confidence crumbled along with my strength. My legs wobbled, and I tasted nothing, not even a salty tear.

In my head, in the setting if Sabrina and I ever had this conversation, I would bawl my eyes out, but the shock of the exchange left me numb. I was devoid of any emotion but a complete emptiness at the loss of my friend.

I slogged my way to the parking garage and my car. I started the engine and my phone rang again. Jordan. I let voice mail shield me.

I don't remember the drive home. I could have hit a pedestrian and drove off down the street without knowing. Part of my world just flooded with truth and washed away into nothingness. Our spacious condo now threatened to smother me. I changed into lightweight jeans and a tank top, leaving the scarf intact to shield my secret once again.

I imagined everyone walking or riding bikes on the canal stared at my secret, but instead, I blended into the fabric of people indulging in the ambiance of a warm summer afternoon. From our condo to the end of the canal stretched a half mile of concrete path. At the point where the sidewalk ended, a bridge connected to the walk on the opposite side. I plopped on the hill in the velvet grass to watch the ducks having their early evening meal.

The buzz of an incoming text displayed Jordan's name on the phone screen. I didn't bother to read the message. I lay back on the grass staring at the fluffy clouds above, imagining what crazy animal the fluff formed, but instead every cloud resembled a bondage toy.

For the fourth time, my ringtone interrupted my misery. I picked up and considered answering Jordan, but instead dropped the phone on the grass beside me. I still wasn't in the mood to talk, so I closed my eyes and relaxed into the comfort of the cool grass. A shadow loomed over me, and I opened my eyes to see my husband glaring down at me.

"What the hell are you doing, Emma?" His voice, not happy, but then again neither was I. I didn't like him much right now, for showing me a source of joy that now caused my grief. I blew out a long and painful sigh. For the second time today, someone I loved called me Emma. Sabrina always called me Jaynie. What a fucked up day.

"I just needed to take a walk." The turmoil in my heart bubbled in my stomach.

"I've been lookin' for you everywhere. You worried the hell out of me. I called and texted, and I know you knew I was on the other end, because I just now watched you look at your phone. You knew it was me. What the hell's going on?"

"Sabrina knows."

"Knows what?" He squatted beside me. His jaw twitched with anger.

"About this." I pointed to my neck.

"You never told her?" He snapped a blade of grass from the ground. "She's your best friend." He stood, running his hands through his hair, leaving a few strands standing as the summer humidity had moistened the hair across his forehead.

"Really, Jordan, how do you explain this scenario? How do you explain to someone her husband has to have leather around his wife's neck?"

"If she were truly your best friend, she'd understand. Did you tell her you like it?"

"Hardly got far into that conversation. She stormed off."

He swiped a hand over his face. "I can't believe you didn't tell her before we got married."

"Well, my life changes are not something I'm comfortable telling people. How many have you told?"

He opened his mouth but hesitated.

"Yeah, I didn't think so," I said.

"Some know. My sister. We're twins you know. Wasn't hard for her to figure out. The people in the playgroup. A lot of people knowing could jeopardize my career."

"Well, Jordan. The fact is, is if I can't keep our secret from her, it's but a matter of time before other people find out. Hell, my co-workers talk behind my back about how they think I've changed. Lori Mays constantly talks about the change when she's not talking about how unbelievable it is you even married me. How long before my work finds out?"

His long black lashes hooded his eyes "I'm sorry you have to go through the upset. They won't find out. Do you think Sabrina'll tell anyone?"

"No. I'm sure she won't. She won't be talking to me anytime soon either." I propped myself up on my elbows. Saying those words deepened the loss like a death.

"Emma. I'm sorry this has hurt you. Good friends aren't easy to come by."

I foresaw a 'but' coming on.

"But, I don't care whether she knows or hates me or you right now. I do care my wife refuses to acknowledge my calls. You always take my calls, *always*."

I'd never seen him red-faced. And if I presumed this was the end of the tirade, I was mistaken.

"I come home, and your car is there, but no Emma. I've spent the last hour walking all over this damn canal looking for you, and you don't give a shit."

He had a point, but I just couldn't deal with him right now. "I had a little more to think about than what the fuck you wanted for dinner. That's why you started calling wasn't it? I don't care. I don't give a shit what we eat for dinner or anything else."

His suit coat twirled as he turned and stomped away from me. "Where're you going?" I yelled after him.

Now, people on the canal turned their attention to Jordan, our very loud exchange, and me.

"To make me something to eat. Answer your god

damn phone next time." His steps pounded so hard, I swear I could hear them on the grass.

I picked the phone from beside me and heaved the one thing I had at him, unaware my aim was spot on. I hit him in the back of the head.

"Ow," he yelped.

Oh, crap.

He whirled around with a furious face. He picked my phone from the grass and dropped the weapon of destruction in his suit jacket pocket. He walked away, his jacket flapping from his speed.

I sat in the same spot for at least another hour, but a real sense of dread weighed heavy on me knowing I had to go home sometime. Even if I wanted to go to my dad's house, my keys to my car were in the condo. Then again, my dad would send me home to talk this out with my husband. On lead feet, I muddled my way home to the lion's den.

When I slipped through the door being as inconspicuous as I could, I found Jordan in different clothes in the kitchen drinking a glass of water.

"I thought you were making dinner?" I couldn't think of anything else to say.

He sat the glass on the counter so hard, I waited for shattering glass to fly around the room. "No, I said I was going to make me something to eat. I made a sandwich. You're on your own," he said.

"Where's my phone?" I asked.

He stepped to the island, bent down and opened the bottom drawer. Without a word, he grabbed a hammer, drew my phone out of his jeans back pocket, unceremoniously set my lifeline on the counter, and proceeded to smash a six hundred dollar phone. Pieces of my life flew in all directions. One fragment beaned me in the forehead.

I shrieked. "What the fuck are you doing? Stop! Why would you do that?"

After returning the hammer to the drawer, his icy calm stare scared the crap of me. "If you're not going to answer, then you don't need a fuckin' phone." He picked up the destroyed pieces of my life and carried the shards to the trash. Electronic particles still lay scattered on the floor.

A new emotion for me—fury. I whipped my hand to the back of my neck ready to undo the collar, but I stopped. The glare from his eyes, the light ice blue now a deep dark of churning ocean, told me if I did tear away the collar our vow to each other, we were finished. Without another word, I stormed to the bathroom to wash my face.

And to cry.

With water dripping from my face, I reached for the towel draped over the rack. Missing. I wiped my face with my hands and still dripping water on the floor, I kneeled to the cabinet to retrieve another towel, when something caught my eye in the bathroom trashcan. A towel lay wadded in the bottom, but the dark stain attracted my attention. I retrieved the towel, examining the stain. Blood. I carried the towel to the kitchen and witnessed Jordan leaning over the counter with his head in his hands.

"Jordan, what is this? What happened?"

He may have lifted his head toward me, but his eyes focused on the towel. "My blood. Your phone cut open my head."

My hands flew to my mouth. "I'm sorry. I'm so

sorry. We should go to the hospital. You might need stitches."

He raised his hand in warning. "It's fine. It's not that bad. I suggest we don't talk right now."

My heart fell to my stomach. I managed to keep my knees from buckling, but not wobbling.

In the span of a few hours, I had lost my best friend and maybe my husband. Revolting couldn't even begin to describe the feeling in my body.

Walking home from the canal that night, I assumed things couldn't get any worse. They got a lot worse. I left the kitchen and headed to our bedroom. Slipping my jeans to a puddle on the floor, I climbed into our bed. Mental exhaustion kept me from the effort of changing into pajamas. At no time during the night did I feel the mattress sink from his weight or his arm around my waist. I didn't get his nightly amusement from the annoying way his finger crisscrossed my shoulder sending power surges of shock straight to my ass. I got nothing and deservedly so.

"Emma. Emma. Wake up."

Still Emma, not Angel.

I opened my eyes to see him standing by the bed ready for work. He finished buttoning his sleeve. "You need to get up to get ready for work."

I rolled to my back, pulling the sheet up to my chin. "I'm not going to work today." I fought the urge to vomit when my hand brushed the cold sheet of an undisturbed side of the bed. Dejection drifted through my body. Yesterday happened that's why.

"Fine." He gathered his jacket lying in perfect trim over the end of the bed.

I closed my eyes, shutting out the reality of the

disdain in my husband's answer.

The condo door slamming rattled my nerves, followed by the devastating silence filling our home, enveloping me in a cocoon of nothing but the ringing in my ears. I flipped the sheet back and searched for my phone on the nightstand. Shit, no phone. I would have to send an e-mail to my boss to tell him I was sick and would not be in the office today. I wasn't lying. Nausea and a killer headache battled for control of my body.

I shuffled into the living room to wake my laptop. The screen welcomed me back. Thanks, but not in the mood. I typed a short and to the point e-mail to my boss, explaining my phone was trashed so I could not call to tell him I was sick. *Just tell Lori Mays she can throw more of her work on my desk.*

Tea and toast to my rescue. I put the mug of water into the microwave before dropping a slice of bread into the toaster. As the toast popped up, and the microwave beeped, the click of a key in the lock stopped me in place. Jordan emerged through the door. As he and his determined materialization advanced toward me, I froze and held my breath, now for uncertainty instead of passion. Scanning his body from toe to the top of his silky head, my heart hurt from the wound I inflicted to his heart. My embarrassment to tell my friend about my life meant one thing.

I was ashamed of our life.

The knot already seeded in my gut grew larger.

"Did you forget something?" I asked. *I'm sorry. I love you so much.*

He said nothing but drove me against the island counter crushing my mouth with his, bruising my lips with his zeal. His hands held my face with such force, I had to surrender to his advance. He raked his hands through my hair, then down to my neck and across the sensitive nerve in my shoulder. Then he lifted me to settle my ass on the cold granite.

"Arms up," he commanded as he pulled my tank top over my head and tossed it aside. I buried my face in his neck, absorbing his citrusy fragrance. He none too gently captured my nipple into his mouth, sucking and biting until I screamed with pleasure from pain of his mouth's grip.

All while I moaned with his torturing of my nipple, I heard him fumbling with his belt and zipper. I lost focus as the sound of him kicking off his shoes on the tile distracted my attention. His belt buckle jingled and crashed to the floor, followed by a *swoosh* as his trousers and underwear followed. He crooked his finger in the waistband of my underwear before ripping them down my legs. I floated with weightlessness as he jerked me off the counter and onto his rock hard dick about to show no mercy in the mission.

And I needed no mercy in the hardest, deepest, and worst way.

I wrapped my legs around his waist, squeezing with his every thrust—faster and deeper he delivered. He managed to hold me with one arm, while using his other hand to fill my core to an excruciating limit. "I can't wait, Jordan. I can't." I choked out the words.

"I don't want you to. Come, Angel. Come with me," he pleaded.

Within seconds of each other, our releases claimed and bonded us once more. He lowered me to the counter with his head buried into the side of my neck. His ragged breath warmed my heart, and again made me ache. I hungered to fuse my body to his so I never experienced the emptiness and ache of an unslept in bed again.

When our breathing had somewhat returned to normal, Jordan trailed more kisses from my neck, finishing on my lips before he broke away. "I can't stay mad you, Angel. I just can't."

I caressed his scalp with my hands until my fingers connected with a crusty wound. "Ow," he flinched.

I jerked away my hand. "I'm so sorry, Jordan."

He put his hand on my lips. "Don't be. I didn't support you when I should have." He grasped my upper arms, holding me at arm's length. "Did you play softball in high school or something?"

"Centerfield. All-State my junior and senior year." I raised a fist. "Go Hawks."

"Well, certainly explains your aim."

"I don't like it when you're mad at me," I said with a sigh. "My biggest fear in getting married was I would disappoint you, and that's what I've been doing."

Jordan caressed my cheeks with his thumbs. "No," he whispered. "No, you aren't disappointing me. Not at all." He teased my lips with but a taste of their warmth. Still, I craved everything he would give.

"We've both made mistakes and will continue to make mistakes. But, Angel, you could never disappoint me. I just think we need some practice in communication. I'm sorry about what happened between you and Sabrina. Give her a few days, maybe she'll want to talk."

My eyes filled with tears. "I don't know if she ever will. If she held a big secret from me, I would be pretty angry, too."

"Are you ashamed of us?" His question harbored a rejection I wanted to shove deep into oblivion.

I traced the line of his lips with my finger and closed my eyes. My embarrassment hurt him I know.

"I'm not ashamed. I just don't know how to accept myself."

I buried my face into his neck again as he wrapped me in his arms and used the wordless embrace as an antidote for the pain. The rhythm of his breathing served as a drug for my tension, and the light citrusy scent of his aftershave induced my desire to relocate this rendezvous to our bed where the leather straps lay anchored. "Are you going to work?" I asked him.

"Well, as much as I'm enjoying this, I need to go to work. I want to go on vacation in two weeks, so I have a lot to get finished before we go." He broke our embrace, and I marveled his shirt didn't even wrinkle through our make-up sex.

I wrapped my arms around his neck. "You still haven't told me where we're going. I don't know what to pack."

His eyes filled with mischief and a smile spread across his face. "Maybe you won't need clothes."

I sat back. "I refuse to go to a nudist camp, beach, or any other exhibitionist venues."

"Damn. You are ruining my surprise."

I think my stunned reaction amused him. "I was kidding. Let me pack for you, and then when we get to the airport, you'll find out. Bring your passport, but that doesn't mean anything. You may or may not need it."

I sighed. "You know I don't have the patience for this kind of thing."

"The very reason why we work on patience."

"No. You make patience training your excuse to torture me."

He smiled, but no denial. He grabbed his wallet from his pants on the floor, pulled out his credit card, and tossed the platinum card on the counter. "Since I broke it, go get yourself a new phone today."

Ordinarily, I preferred to pay for my own big purchases, but he was right, he was the one who broke my phone. Despite the fact, he wouldn't have if I had answered him. Holding grudges occupied my DNA not his. Neither did I have his optimism for Sabrina's forgiveness.

Two weeks later, Sabrina still wouldn't talk to me, and my career faced a huge challenge.

Chapter Thirteen

Sitting with my back against the headboard—the rod iron rails imprinted against my kidneys like a freezing sword. Jordan began his exploration. On his stomach with his arms around my waist, he warmed me, but not like normal. Even with his tantalizing tongue roaming around my naval, I couldn't appreciate his effort to ignite my arousal. Physically, I couldn't have been in a better, more loving place. Mentally, I was lost in a maze of confusion and self-doubt.

Jordan had established this night and him as a no-touch zone, but I needed to experience the tactile connection between us. I needed to touch him to keep me from thinking about my day. My hands eased across the muscled landscape of his back, rubbing in circles around his shoulder blades. The simple action released the tension of my nightmare day.

He stopped his oral fondling of my belly. "Angel, you keep forgetting. Do that again, and I'll tie your hands to the bed." His light-hearted tone thinly disguised the rule reminder.

I flung my hands underneath my butt, and Jordan's mouth descended on my nipple. Unable to take what I needed, I started to tremble, and I couldn't stop the tears. They dripped from my cheek onto Jordan's shoulder. He stilled and raised his head. Seeing my tears, he scrambled to my side, before wiping a trail from my cheek. "Angel, what's wrong, baby?"

I couldn't hold my anguish in any longer. "I got fired," I said in a ragged breath.

Jordan wrapped his arms around my shaking shoulders. "What?"

"I got fired today." The waterfall of tears spilled, so I wrapped my arms around his neck. He squeezed me tight, letting the sobs release the broken pieces of my life. After a few minutes, I wriggled from his embrace in a futile effort to compose myself.

"What happened?" he asked.

Between sniffles, I explained. "In legal terms, I was downsized, but everyone knows it's because not a day goes by Lori Mays and I are not at each other's throats."

"Was she let go also?" he asked.

"No."

"Why just you?"

"I'm not sleeping with Gary Johnson, the company president." I'd never be desperate enough.

"Oh, I see. Why don't you two get along?" With his lips on my temple and arms around my naked body, I had my own personal heating pad emitting a smell like a day at the beach.

"It's been going on a long time. She's lazy and doesn't know how to do her job and pawns her work off on me. Ever since we got married, she's just been riding me about my new taste in clothes. She thinks I'm lying about being married to someone as hot as you. I told her she didn't need to comment about my clothes since I never commented on how she dressed like a hooker or sucked Johnson's dick." My mouth, a constant source of conflict had struck again.

"I hammered my own nail in the coffin. I'm sure she went straight to Johnson, because today, all of a sudden, the market is down. The company is tightening their belts and cutting costs."

"Hmm, I'm sorry." He squeezed me tighter.

"I have to have a job. I still have a college loan to finishing paying off," I said. Four more years, and I would be debt free from a degree I wasn't even using. Yay.

He palmed my cheek. "I can pay. Don't worry."

"No!" My forceful rebuff projected a spray of moisture across his cheek. "It's my debt to pay, not yours. I don't want you paying for me." I was no princess. I paid my own bills. Though I was heartened he offered.

His eyes widened, the back of his hand wiped the spit from his face.

"I appreciate you offering, but no," I added.

He kissed my forehead. I think he understood my need to support myself. "Did you love your job? Was it your dream job?"

"No." Not even close."

"Did you even like your job?"

"Well, not lately," I answered. "The last few months, I kind of hated going in to work, but this was my job and, not to sound arrogant, I was good. I can't be without a job."

He brushed the hair from my face and kissed my forehead again. "Well, then try and think of this as a good thing, an opportunity. You may not have left the job on your own, because you believed you had to have any job. Now, you can do something else. Different company, different job, or even a different career if you want."

"Not many publishers in this city." How many times would I change careers? I needed some stability. Teaching was a bust. Now editing was a no go. Quickmart sounded very appealing right now. Punch a clock, ring up bread, and go home.

"Don't limit yourself. Wanna work at my company?" he asked.

I was naked sitting on his naked lap, and he didn't even have a hard on. How pathetic was I? "Oh yeah, so then I would be the one sleeping with the boss. I don't think so."

"Why don't you try writing? You've a lot experience with fiction."

"Sure. I'm good at telling people they aren't using commas correctly. I don't have thick enough skin for someone to tell me what's wrong with mine. No book writing for me."

"Whatever is supposed to be there for you will happen. Trust me, I know everything." I caught his eye roll and attempt at humor." In the meantime, just collect your unemployment and enjoy some time off—unless you want to file a lawsuit for wrongful termination."

"Nope. You're right. I didn't even like what I was doing of late. I wouldn't sue to get a job back I don't even want. It's...It's a shock. I've never been fired. Have you?"

He flashed those perfect teeth. "Yeah, I have, a few times."

"No shit?"

His eyebrows furrowed.

"In high school, I got fired from my first job because after the fifth time of oversleeping and being late, the owner of the Curly Cone said I either needed to stop partying all night or find a different job."

"So did you find another job?"

"I went to work for my dad's landscaping business. Immediately put an end to the partying all night."

"What about the other time?" I asked.

"My first job out of college I worked for an advertising firm in Louisville. I failed to put some important meetings on the calendar, and when the clients showed up, no one was ready for them, and we lost the accounts. I lost my job."

"So what did you do?"

"I moved back to Indy. Got my job here, as an admin assistant to a communications director and moved on from there with the painful lessons I'd learned. So, everything works out in the end. If those things hadn't happened, I wouldn't have what I have now. Every misstep leads us to the place we're supposed to be…here with you."

"I hate you are so much smarter than I am," I confessed. Why couldn't I see what he did?

"I'm not in the least. I've just had my hard knocks sooner in life than you did."

I rested my head on his bare chest, listening to his heart and breathing in his soothing scent. I could stay this way forever since I no longer had a job.

"Hey," Jordan lifted my chin with his hand. "Why didn't you tell me this when I got home today?"

Because I thought if I didn't tell you, it wouldn't be real. Because I thought I was a failure. Because I thought you would think I was a loser. "Because I was embarrassed."

"Don't be." His thumb and forefinger squeezed my

chin for my attention. "You aren't a failure. You aren't a loser. You're terrific."

Fuck. How did he get into my brain? Can he read minds? Well the 'terrific' part never entered my internal conversation, but having my mind read was fucking scary.

"It's just a job, Emma, not who you are."

I released the breath I had been holding for hours. "What am I going to do tomorrow?"

Jordan nudged me back onto the bed. "I don't know, but I know what we're going to do now... And you may use your hands until I find those straps."

Chapter Fourteen

Since I hadn't found a job in the last month, I adjusted, though not whole-heartedly, to my new role as proverbial housewife. I cleaned, ran errands, cooked. Flat out, my life was hell. I had trouble saying *domestic*, let alone implementing the routine.

Once I'd finished my chores, I spent the balance of the day using every means I had to scramble for a new job. Thanks to the gossip wheel at Millennial, I now had a reputation in the small world of local publishers as "not a team player." In other words, if I had "done the team," then maybe I would still have a job, but no self-respect.

The student loan people didn't care about my self-respect, only their investment, and right now, the outgoing money drained my savings account and unemployment didn't cover the monthly payment.

Desperation and the future of my credit report forced me to ask my husband for help.

Jordan did everything to make me feel better. He even ramped up our sexual experimentation—the positions left me exhausted and falling into a coma-like slumber. However, once the morning arrived, the dismal reality returned.

But still, I was jobless.

Summer morphed to an early fall, and the frosty chill and the darkness of November descended on me like a suffocating plastic trash bag.

Even though Jordan arrived home at the same time as in the summer, the early darkness tricked my mind into thinking he was spending much more time at work.

When he walked through the door every night, he hugged away my fears, and he was extra attentive, making my mundane daily existence important.

I stifled a gasp in my throat one night watching him remove his black leather gloves as one of the most erotic things I had ever seen. I know he wasn't consciously trying to arouse me. He talked about his day and finger by finger, he tugged on the glove until loose enough to pull from his hand. So captivated by the simple action, I forgot to breathe when he started on the second one. Overwhelmed with simple, but raging lust, I wanted those hands in sleek black leather touching me wrong in all the right places.

"Earth to Angel," he roused me from my fantasy. "Where are you? You seem a little out there."

"Sorry, just wandered away somewhere in my mind." I plastered a huge smile on my face. "I'm back."

Nope. Still fantasizing about those gloves.

I continued to stare at the gloves lying on the granite counter. I picked them up, fondling the soft leather in my hands. *Whoa.*

The discomfort between my legs expanded to pain throughout my body. My descent into slutdom happened way sooner than I expected. I had way too much time on my hands with little to think about except what I wanted from my husband.

"I'm going to change." He shrugged from his black wool car coat and hung it in the hall closet. He disappeared into our bedroom. I so wanted to follow, but the sizzle from the chicken in the skillet made me act like a responsible person and stay on point.

When Jordan returned to the kitchen, he had changed from his suit trousers to jeans but left on his black cashmere turtleneck sweater. Oh dear God, I couldn't draw a normal breath when he wore it. "You cold?" I asked trying to sound not in the least turned on.

"A little. I'm having a hard time readjusting to the cold weather again."

"Weeewell," I stuttered. "Since I have so much more free time now, I made your favorite, banana pudding for dessert."

His eyes sparkled at the mention of homemade banana pudding.

During dinner, I dropped my fork on the floor twice. My bare leg throbbed from the hot mashed potatoes that missed my mouth and plopped onto my thighs from to my lap. When Jordan suggested I go get ready for bed, I practically bolted from the table. I brushed my hair, my teeth, and ripped off my clothes. The dim light from the bedside table created a warm glow in the room.

Feeling the change in the air of the bedroom, I quavered with anticipation. When firm, but gentle hands grasped my waist, I froze. I say hands, but familiar hands encased in supple deerskin gloves. When the slick texture of the pliant leather caressed my stomach, I fought to keep myself standing.

"You know, you're not very subtle," he whispered in my ear. "You were watching me, and I discerned with no problem what you wanted. You wanted this." One hand rested on my belly just above my naval, while the other, *Oh my God,* creeped along to my breast where he circled one gloved finger around my nipple. I drew a long breath, moaning deep in my throat. The sensation of the leather rubbing my nipple sent an electrical shock through my breast. Each motion sent a wave of new leather scent through my nose, and I was about to come undone.

Shit. Shit. Keep silent. No cussing in the bedroom.

"Shit, Jordan." The word slipped from my tongue in a whisper I hoped he didn't hear.

"I'll let you pass this time." But he squeezed my nipple hard enough that I squealed and shuddered.

Both of his hands slid up and down my sides, circling, caressing, and squeezing my skin. He continued to my collarbone, and then rested the soft leather on my shoulders. The compelling aroma opened the door to vivid memories of leather cuffs holding me hostage while Jordan tormented me into freaky volatile orgasms. How things had changed. No longer scared of being bound or commanded, but yet the anticipation of what might transpire both unnerved and exhilarated me.

"You like?"

"Fu..." I remembered the language thing. "Holy Hell, I so love what you're doing." I didn't exactly consider "Hell," to be cussing.

He began massaging my shoulders, teasing my arousal, but relaxing my body. I wasn't sure I could stand on my own anymore, so I leaned my body into his chest where I met the feathery threads of the cashmere. Leather and cashmere attacking my skin from both sides and working in unison sending my brain and body into maximum of "I don't know what the fuck is happening, but I don't want to stop."

When he put his right hand fingers over my mouth,

I admit, in my head, I got a little scared, but the dangerous side of me almost came on the spot. I was getting better at holding on to a climax, but this sweet torture challenged my resolve.

Keeping his hand on my mouth, his other hand compressed against my neck, sending drops of sizzling fireworks zigzagging from my neck to my toes before setting up camp in the happiest place on earth. All this while his thumb stroked my jawline. A slow moan deep in my throat forced its way between his fingers.

"Do you like me holding you like this?" His voice now dark and salacious—this sound from a stranger would set off every alarm bell in the tower. His lips brushed my ear before taking the soft lobe in his teeth. His hand clamped so tight against my mouth, I could only nod my acceptance. I was quite sure he would give me another pass so I didn't verbalize my answer.

"My sweet Angel," he whispered, trapping me in so many ways. He imprisoned my head with his strength, but emotionally, my mind dived into a barrel of warm fudge. *Let me drown.* I never wanted out of his soft, gooey, velvety feeling filling my body and only stopped for the mere reason I ran out of toes.

I let out a moan of protest when he released me, but as soon as he let go, he hoisted me over his shoulder to continue the sweet torture in our bed.

"I want you to touch me, Angel," he said standing over me and dominating my vision right before he pulled the sweater over his head.

I get to touch. "Maybe I should make banana pudding more often."

Jordan closed his eyes shaking his head. He wasn't mad. He was trying to keep from laughing.

When he tore off the sweater exposing his chest, I couldn't help but marvel at how ridiculously handsome my husband was. Mine, all mine. I would let him do anything, and I meant anything, at this moment, but I was getting the biggest treat of the night...He was going to let me touch him as much as I wanted without waiting for permission.

Who knew such a little thing was orgasmic.

The hair on his chest and arms tickled and scratched, his smell of winter wind mixed with the soapy fragrance of summer invaded my nose, and the heat of his body tested and rewarded all of me. But my touching of him, restored my soul, soothed my frazzled mind, and melted my heart.

When Jordan joined me on the bed, he still wore the gloves and the black silk ropes which dangled from his left hand. Confusion raised its hand.

"You said I could touch you?"

"You can. You just have to find a way without your hands."

Wait. What?

I offered no resistance as he grasped my hands and tied them to the black iron rails. "I don't understand."

In the low light of the room, I still could make out his smile. "Use your delectable little body."

He made an impossible request, but the more he caressed my skin with those gloves, the higher I arched my back into his delectable big body. Again, the smell of the leather encompassed me when he cupped my face with both hands. His grip rendered me paralyzed, and I pulled at the restraints in a pointless attempt to free my hands.

Sometimes I was not so fond of the lessons Jordan

taught me. As he assaulted my face with his not so gentle lips, I chased his body with mine. My stomach pressed hard into his. My legs curled and uncurled around his calves while his coarse black hairs fashioned a scouring pad to my skin, and I ached with his unspoken promise to fill me in all ways.

"Jordan?" was the extent of my words as he released my face, but covered my mouth with his gloved hand, sending me crazy with arousal, and I bucked against his hips on mine. About five seconds after he slipped his cock inside of me, I let loose, too late realizing my mistake.

Oops.

Jordan's gaze bored into me at my failure to hold back. "I guess we are just going to have to do start all over again," he whispered still with his hand clamped over my mouth. I shook my head no. I couldn't bear this sweet agony again. Removing his hand, his leather-wrapped finger found its way into my core.

"Oh yes, my Angel who flies too fast, we're doing this again."

Chapter Fifteen

Rubbing the corner of her eyes, Jessica cocked her head, I suppose studying my face for answers to an unknown question.

"Is something wrong?" I asked.

"Not at all. Again, I'm fascinated. You said you were hesitant and apprehensive at first about living with BDSM, but seems to me, you've adjusted without much conflict."

I bit my lower lip. "Well, no, I wouldn't say that."

****

God, he was getting on my nerves. For the third time this week, Jordan's brand of domination had little to do with bondage and more to do with keeping me from satisfaction. Oh, don't get me wrong. I had my releases, but after, I had jumped through every one of his proverbial hoops. No cussing, or even better, no talking. No touching unless given permission. "Just feel, Angel. I'll do everything you need. Just listen to what I say." *Bite me*.

He did bite, but I was so frustrated, the stinging pinches pissed me off instead of the usual driving me to the edge of insanity. More than once, he told me I wasn't being submissive with my back talk. The translation was I wasn't good enough to be his submissive. I wasn't good enough to be employed, and I wasn't good enough to satisfy my husband.

After we'd finished, Jordan told me to sit up against the headboard. The sheet lay across my lap, but the rest of my naked body awaited his next order. My nipples pebbled from the cool air in the room and his recent manipulation with his tongue. He licked the crevasse between my breasts and while any other day, his tongue on my body set me on fire, but today, right then, I just wanted a shower.

"Are we really going to do this again?" I was not sure what he assumed he would hear, but the words slipped from my mouth before I could halt them.

He stopped and raised his head to meet my gaze. He raised his eyebrows but said nothing. When my belly growled, he rubbed his hand against my stomach. "I guess you're grumpy because you need something to eat." He jerked himself away and left our bed walking toward the kitchen ruffling his hair with his hands as he shook his head.

His rules held me in place. His rules slapped my face, and I seethed with anger. I had no control over anything in my life.

Jordan returned with a plate of cheese, ham, crackers, strawberries, and sliced bananas. All of my favorite after-scene snacks. He sat on the edge of the bed, and I attempted to pick a strawberry from the plate.

He slapped away my hand and frowned.

"Why are you having such trouble today?"

I shrugged.

He grabbed the strawberry, raising the unwanted fruit to my lips. "Open."

I hesitated just long enough to watch his eyes darken. I opened my mouth, accepting the sweet berry. This time, he gave me a banana, followed by another strawberry and a cube of Colby cheese.

When he lifted another strawberry to my lips, I shook my head. "I don't want any more."

"Angel, you've hardly eaten anything in the last few days."

I stiffened and knocked away the plate. Cheese, fruit, and crackers flipped onto the mattress. "I don't want anymore." My jaw ached from gritting my teeth so hard.

I threw my legs over the side of the bed and stomped into the bathroom. Why had such a simple act sent me over the edge?

Turning on the faucet, I waited for the water to warm. I needed a hot shower to release my tension.

Stepping into the steam, I could barely see the porcelain tile in the cloud of moisture. I faced the stream, letting the hot water roll down my hair, face, breasts, and trembling body. Hearing a click, I cocked my head, but instead of identifying the sound, I identified the strong hands caressing my shoulders.

When he kissed the back of my neck, my nerves rebelled, and I froze.

"Jordan, stop."

He continued his kiss, nipping my skin, while his hands grasped my breasts. "Shhh. Just be still."

I flung my arm backward trying to dislodge his touch. "Stop, Jordan. Just stop and leave me alone."

From the corner of my eye, I caught sight of surrendered hands as he exited the shower. The slamming of the bathroom door rang through my ears and stunned my brain. I didn't even know if he grabbed a towel.

As soon as he left, my heart sank, and a huge knot

grew in my stomach. *What did I just do?* Once the first tear dropped, I lost all control and the sobs released like a broken dam. Who was I anymore? Had I so wrapped myself in Jordan's needs, I disappeared?"

I had no job.

I depended on my husband for everything.

My best friend hadn't spoken to me in months.

The subject of all of those sentences was me, and I had to accept the responsibility. Jordan had nothing to do with my depression. He was just the spark who ignited my explosion.

Shivering from the now cold water, I shut off the water.

The sobbing ceased.

I toweled off, wrapped my robe around me, and forced myself to stand before the love of my life to apologize for being such a shit.

I found him collapsed in the overstuffed leather recliner. His headed rested against the back. His eyes were closed, exposing the lush brown lashes I lusted over. When I climbed into his lap, his hands gathered at my waist and steadied my position.

The frosty feel of his hands confirmed the climate of this scene—desolate.

My wet hair already curled about my shoulders. I leaned forward to kiss his forehead. Jordan remained silent—his expression unreadable.

I panicked. The blood in my veins thickened, and my heart shattered at his distance. I loved this man. I desired everything he did to me, but today, I shunned him.

I searched his eyes for forgiveness, but what reflected in the icy blue scared me.

Detachment.

"Jordan, I'm sorry. I didn't mean…It's just…" The tears arrived. I brushed away the hair plastered across my cheek. "I…"

He drew me into his chest, crushing my shoulders with his embrace. "It's all right."

I sniffed. "No, nothing is all right."

I raised my head away from his drumming heart. Looking into the eyes I expected to soothe me instead scared me. The playfulness I was used to seeing now shimmered with a sad moisture.

Brushing his beautiful hair from his forehead, I think I held my breath at least five minutes before explaining my ridiculous reason for hurting him.

"Jordan, the last few months have just overwhelmed me. First, I never knew my mom. You know I told you she died when I was just a baby. So, my whole life, Sabrina has been my rock. I told her everything."

Jordan opened his mouth, but I stopped any words with my fingers to his lips. "Please, just let me finish before you say anything."

I wanted to slip my finger into his mouth, but now, the time for carefree play had vanished when I dismissed my husband like an unruly puppy. "I know I was completely at fault for not telling her, but still, losing her…I just can't accept she's gone from my life."

Shifting my weight in his lap, I waited for the familiar bulge to grow, but nothing. "Then I lost my job." His eyebrows rose. "I know. I know. I didn't like the job anymore, but at least I had an identity. I had some responsibility. I made decisions. Now, I'm dependent on you." I blew out a heavy breath. "I can't even pay my bills or contribute anything."

I rested my head against his shoulder, fingering the smooth skin over his breast. "Then we get into the bedroom, and still I have no say in anything. You wouldn't let me touch you, and I needed to touch you. I needed to feel every hot hair on your body to reassure me I still exist. Some days, I just don't believe I even exist."

Pulling his chin toward me, I kissed his forehead, tasting his skin with the tip of my tongue. "Jordan, I love what you do to me, but today I couldn't, and I'm sorry. I never want to hurt you."

"Emma…"

Emma. Not Angel, but Emma. I fought to hold the tears at bay.

I wanted to be Angel. Right now. I didn't like Emma because of what she just did to make her husband feel so rejected.

Jordan cupped my face with his hands—hands, which always delivered me to an exhausting and exhilarating release. The chill remained and was not replaced with the tender heat I always expected.

"Emma. I didn't realize you were so down. I failed you. I should recognize when you're hurting."

He rested his cold forehead against mine, but instead of relaxing with reassurance, I shivered with dread. I didn't want to hear the words about to fall from his mouth.

"We struggle with communicating…a lot, and communicating is a foundation for a relationship. We've failed each other. I wanted to be a Dominant to you, but I clearly didn't do my job in understanding your needs."

Yes. Yes. I love how you are my Dominant.

He absorbed my complications as his deficiencies. Jordan blamed himself for my insecurities. How had this conversation gone so wrong?

"I wanted this to work, but it's not." He tipped my chin, forcing me to connect my tear-filled eyes to his own. "I'm not going to live like this. We're done. It's not gonna work."

Done? No…

Chapter Sixteen

"Whoa," Jessica dropped her pen. It bounced from the laptop to the floor. "I did not see that coming."

Even now, as I related the story, my eyes filled with tears. As he spoke the words, the deep regret he couldn't hide stabbed at my heart.

The day.

Even though I survived and emerged stronger. I'll remember the day for the rest of my life.

Every action has a consequence. When I had my meltdown, in no way did I anticipate the conclusion.

"It's still sounds painful?" Jessica's voice interrupted my flashback roaming.

I pulled my legs to the cushion and draped my arms around my knees. Resting my chin on my kneecaps, I said. "It is. We worked on control and patience. While I was so much better, I couldn't separate me, the submissive, from me the depressed, unemployed, lost my best friend, didn't know what to do, woman."

She squinted her eyes and raised a finger. "But you're wearing a collar. Obviously, something good happened." Retrieving her pen from the floor, Jessica still wore the shock on her face when she sat up again.

I shrugged. "My actions ended that relationship. I'm in a different relationship now, and I'm gloriously happy in this one."

"What changed? What's different in this one?"

I closed my eyes thinking about the man behind the door with the scruffy face. "Everything I needed to change."

"I bet that made you pretty happy," Jessica smiled as she chewed the end of her pen. "

"Like finding a waterhole in the desert."

"So happily ever after then...no going back to vanilla?"

Vanilla? She knew a few things about kink.

"Went vanilla for a while but turned out to be a disaster."

A chill in the air made me shiver so I snatched up my sweater and drew my protection over my head, once again covering any evidence of my life. I caught Jessica eyeing me like I talked out of both sides of my mouth. "I tend to be cold natured. I don't get freaked out by what I wear now, but other people do. So, I cover when I wear this one."

Pulling my hair from the back of the turtleneck, I said. "Once I realized my true self, I'm happier now more than ever."

Jessica continued to write allowing me to reflect some more. That life had ended, but as excruciating as the decision was, if we hadn't ended, I never would have found this amazing fulfillment.

"You haven't talked much about your husband now."

"I think the better story is about the journey."

"All right. I've a few more questions," Jessica said.

Sure, but I'm about finished. I'm not normally much of a talker. *Liar. You just want what's behind door number one.*

"Can you be a little more specific about what's different in this relationship?"

What's different? Wow, the pictures in my mind flashed to life in vivid deliciousness. I almost blushed. "Rules and repercussions."

I detected a keen hint of interest in Jessica's face.

"So, you break a rule and you get…punished?"

If I didn't know better, I'd think Jessica was about to experience her own orgasm. With each rise and fall of her chest, she typed with ferocity. When she finished, she took a deep breath. Her cheeks flushed crimson. "So do you get punished often?"

"Hmmm." I bit my lip in concentration. "Not a lot, but sometimes I do things to piss him off just to bring on the discipline."

Her jaw dropped. "Wow? Why would you do that? Punishment doesn't sound very appealing."

A dreamy sigh escaped my mouth. "It can be appealing. When you're restricted, the mind is a powerful tool. I mean, I learned how to control an orgasm…most of the time…but I also learned to have one without being touched. Sometimes the more uncomfortable he makes me, the more intense the orgasm. He has to keep finding ways of punishing me without me getting off on his creativity."

Jessica laughed as she wrote a few more notes. "So punishment kind of backfires."

"In a way. It's more of a game to me than anything. With one word I can take my ball and go home at any time. But, I play through because, it's become my favorite fantasy sport."

"Have you ever safeworded?"

My knees started to ache so I switched to cross-legged sitting. "A few times. Both for physical reasons. Once I came down with the stomach flu, and vomit kind of ruins the moment. Another time, I thought I was healed from a surgery, but once I was tied, I wasn't healed."

"Did he get mad?"

"Not at all. You use a safeword because you need to. Game over, no consequences. Trust and love make safewords, safe words."

Jessica stopped typing and stared. Maybe she was searching for a hint of deception or insanity, or maybe she was jealous. I smiled not at her, but to me inside. I wished everyone could experience the extraordinary physical sensations I do. I'm sure there are other avenues, but I believe my street is paved with gold.

I had to change positions again. Damn knee surgery. "My husband would never dream of hurting me. Everything he does to me is completely safe and also what I want."

"Anything he wants you're not in to?"

"A few things. I'm not comfortable with doing things in public places. I'm terrified someone will jump out of the bushes or walk by. A lot of risk for me. I don't get how public's fun."

She tapped her pen on the laptop in three-quarter time and studied the non-existent pattern on the carpet. When she glanced my way, her peculiar gaze told me she had the willies about something.

"What about…what about…anal sex?"

I think I had the same reaction the first time I understood the reality. "I've done it. Not my favorite by any stretch, and I mean stretch."

She giggled and closed the laptop. Yes. The finish

line. All this talking about my sexual life had aroused me so much I'd begun to squirm. My husband was in for a long night.

After she packed her bag, Jessica slid it to the floor. "Just one more thing, I find your choice of aliases to be rather odd. It doesn't matter, I won't be using your names anyway, but why not Smith, Brown, Jones...the usual?"

I uncrossed my legs and placed my feet flat on the floor without thinking of the result. My right knee commenced the familiar, but unwanted bouncing. My squirming now had little to do with being horny. "Oh that. Those names are pretty boring, don't you think?" I had this. "Last night, I was watching a crime program, and the detective's name was Caldera. The name sounded cool."

I wasn't lying. I did watch the show and about fell on the floor when I heard the detective's name. I didn't want to hurt him now with my story. I believed hiding in plain sight was the best idea.

"Certainly makes things interesting." She stood, slung the bag strap over her shoulder, and folded her jacket under her arm. "This has been enlightening and entertaining. I can't give you a date when the story will run, but I'll let you know."

I stood to walk her to the door. I think I'd lost ten pounds of stress once we finished. "Sorry for the black ops stuff. You know people can overreact, and I don't want anyone to be hurt by what I've said."

She stopped walking, and I almost ran into her back. "That reminds me. Did you ever reconcile with your friend?"

"Sadly, no."

After she left, I leaned against the heavy door mirroring my own heavy heart when I counted how much time had passed since I last spoke with Sabrina. Another part of my life over.

Chapter Seventeen

I didn't even knock before the door to the bedroom opened. He grabbed my arm and yanked me into the room. His furnace of a body rode me hard against the wall. The face of my hero burned with desire all for me, and I trembled as I stroked the coarse hair on his jaw. All of my anxiety faded into history. "It's over. I did it, and I'm so relieved. Now, how about you give me a poke in those fancy sheets?"

He wore nothing but his jeans, and I still marveled at how hot his bare chest made me.

Sweat trickled down my back and popped on my arms turning the soft cashmere into an itchy mess. I pulled the sweater over my head, but his hands then trapped my wrists against the wall.

"What are you doing?"

"I'm trying to get undressed. Problem for you, Sir?"

"No. No. Just slow down. We have all night."

He finished the job, sliding my tank off and undoing my bra—throwing both into the pile forming at my feet. On the other side of the door, I controlled everything about the interview. As soon as he opened the bedroom door, I relinquished everything with no regrets, no hesitation, and no fear.

He ripped the pins holding my wig in place, threw the fake glasses across the room, and stripped away another part of the woman I was. "I'll not a fuck a stranger," he said.

His fingers massaged my sweat-drenched scalp, and the tingling sensation his fingers created almost buckled my knees. With him so close, the woodsy scent of soap invaded my nostrils.

"Why didn't you tell her everything? You wanted to tell your story." His breath tickled my ear, but the inquisition broke the moment. "I was listening at the door in case you're wondering."

"I don't know," I said.

"I don't know is rarely the honest answer."

I inhaled a deep breath, taking his scent with me. Something wasn't right. "You know, I don't like that scent on you."

From my ear to cocking his head in my face, exasperation blossomed. "You're the one who bought it for me."

"I know. I like it on other people, but on you, Jordan, I want my familiar oceany smell."

"What do you mean by 'other' people?" His eyebrows knitted together and the word explanation emerged all over his face.

Let us pray. Please let it be correct men don't notice the smell of other men.

"I smelled it on someone in the store, and I wanted to smell the scent on you, but I don't like it. I want my Mr. Caldera to smell like he always does. However, I do like the non-shaving Jordan."

He got a lot of exercise out of eye rolling. "Damn, Angel. Don't be asking other men about their smell."

I squeaked a little when he gathered my hair into a ponytail and pulled until I had no choice but to look at his eyes. I think I dodged a bullet. As good as Cameron smelled, he'd never be Jordan.

"You're a master of deflecting questions, but I'm not letting this go. Why didn't you tell her the real story? You told her we got divorced."

My finger of correction rocketed into his chest. "There's where you're wrong. I told her *that* relationship ended, and I'm in a new one. I'm not lying, Jordan. Our original relationship did end, but the one we have now is so much better. I just wanted to keep the rest of our story to myself, between us."

A slow smile creeped across his features and those penetrating eyes projected nothing but affection. "I've an idea. Come on."

Without hesitation, I followed him to the bed still in pristine hotel condition. Three hours and three hundred dollars later, we got to see what one thousand thread count sheets do to a body.

I started to unbutton my jeans, but he snatched away my hand. "Nope. We're going to do something else."

"Jordan." I didn't mean to sound like I was whining, but I was.

He patted the front pocket of his jeans. "Don't make me use this."

A resigned sigh escaped my mouth.

"Let's get into bed."

Once we settled against the headboard with me wrapped between his arms and legs, I wondered and worried about the plan.

"Now, since you didn't tell her, I want you to tell me the rest of the story."

What?

"Jordan you were there, you know the rest of the story."

He kept fingering my collar. It'd been a while since I'd worn this one, and with every stroke on the leather, I got wetter, and he got bigger.

"I know the story from my point of view, not yours. I'm sure it's very different. I know my feelings. I don't know yours."

I didn't want to go there with him. It was both painful and embarrassing.

"You don't have to look at me. Just tell me. Everything. No matter if it hurts or is embarrassing."

Fuck me. How does he do that?

Chapter Eighteen

I closed my eyes. Part of the reason I didn't tell Jessica was because I didn't want to relive the day I destroyed us. Maybe he needed to hear it…

"We're done with this lifestyle. It's not working, and I'm losing you."

"But, Jordan…"

This time he covered my lips with his fingers. "Emma. This isn't a time to argue with me." I couldn't hide the look of terror he had to have distinguished in my eyes. "We'll be okay. No one ever died because they couldn't bind up their partner."

With a silent action, he settled his hand behind my neck, slipping the excess strap of my collar through the buckle. I straightened from the slight tightening as he tugged the catch from the hole, and then a cold nakedness when from the jingle of the collar as he dropped my life to the ground.

We sat in silence, for what I believed to be hours, just breathing.

No words.

Plastered to my husband's chest, with free rein to touch and roam, I sprayed my fingers across his heart, feeling his steady beats. How could his heart be so calm when mine tarried a mere seconds from bursting?

"Emma, you need to get up."

"Am I crushing you?"

"No, baby, not at all. I want us to get dressed."

"Why?"

He kissed me, but the pressure indicated he wanted me off. "Because I want to take you to dinner."

I slid from his lap and extended my hands. He grasped both and allowed me to haul him from the chair. "Where do you want to go?"

"I want to go to Ernies."

"Ernies? Why."

Jordan brushed away my still damp and curly hair from my shoulders. My robe fell open, exposing my leg and most of my breasts. "I want to take you to the place where I fell in love with you," he said.

I couldn't breathe for the lump stuck in my throat. The first tear trickled from my eyes, but the rest stampeded like a herd of buffalo. Wrapping my arms around his neck, I sobbed an ugly girl sob.

"Angel, don't cry. You're making too much of this."

Angel...I needed to hear her name. She still lived in me, and Jordan calmed her panic.

"I guess I didn't need to be in the shower with you because you're getting me all wet now." He squeezed me tight, burying his nose in my hair.

Chapter Nineteen

Our relationship changed.

Even though he said nothing would change, the high velocity fuse connecting us fizzled.

The wheel of our daily lives turned as always. Jordan worked. I looked for a job with no success. We ate dinner, watched TV, laughed about the silly things we always laughed about.

We made love.

We were strangers in the same bed. My husband touched me in all the right places, but I sensed a tentativeness in his manner. He allowed me to touch him anywhere, everywhere, and my newfound freedom should have empowered me.

I hated it.

We were two married people who had vanilla sex. So was this what getting old was like? Had our future arrived thirty years too soon?

The strangest thing of all? I missed my black leather band hugging my neck. I missed the constant reminder of who dominated my world. Sub conscientiously, I fingered the area where my collar had embraced me and given me the power and freedom to accept who I was. The smoothness of my neck irritated me, and one day, I tied a familiar scarf around my neck to comfort me. Instead, I fell deeper into a depression.

After three weeks of our new life, I could see

Jordan and me slipping away from each other.

****

I threw up daily. Three pregnancy tests later, I resolved the issue to a bad case of nerves. I couldn't continue to live like this.

As usual, Jordan sauntered through the door with a smile on his face and a deep kiss for me. He asked me about my day. Same as usual, no leads on a job, and a guy won two cars on The Price is Right.

"Jordan?" I hopped on top of the counter and dangled my legs. At this level, I could almost look him square in the eyes. "I want to talk about something."

He made a formidable picture dressed for work. His clothes hugged his broad shoulders and lean waist. His deep brown hair shined under the kitchen lights, and as usual, one chunk of hair flopped over his forehead.

"Let me go change, and we'll talk."

"No, I can't wait. I'll lose my nerve."

His gaze narrowed, and a hard swallow cascaded down his throat.

"All right. What's wrong?"

He leaned into me, placing his hands on the counter on the outside of my thighs. The rhythmic tapping of his fingers on the counter sounded like drums.

I covered my lips with my fingers, unsure how to start. Looking to the floor, then to my husband, I just blurted the words out. "I can't do this anymore, Jordan."

"Do what?"

I brushed his hair from his forehead, to watch it win the battle and return. "I can't live this vanilla life

185

anymore. A year ago, I never knew what the word meant, and now I despise the sound." I cupped his smooth cheeks—his eyes widening as I ran the pads of my thumbs across his cheekbones. "I love you. I'll love you forever but I miss who we were. I miss you binding me, and how I feel when I struggle against those ropes. I miss you telling me what to do and what not to do. I miss you forbidding me to touch you." I placed my forehead on his, feeling the heat exchange between us. "I miss wearing my collar. I miss my connection with you."

Jordan broke our touch, standing upright. I held my breath as he gathered my hair at the back of my neck.

"Angel, you know it wasn't working. I wasn't good enough expressing to you what we needed in order to make this type of relationship work. This was my fault. My failure."

"But Jordan…"

He held his hand up. "I understand what you're saying because don't think I haven't noticed this distance between us." His legs forced my thighs apart to close the space between us. We embraced as if we had lost each other in the desert and found us again. "I don't want to lose us, either."

We remained motionless, lost in each other's pounding hearts. I said what I had to say, and now I waited for Jordan to direct our future. If we stayed this way, we had a difficult hurdle to jump.

As he pulled away, I held my breath, waiting to hear our fate.

"Angel, we can't go back."

I just died.

"We have to do things differently. Very different."

"Are you saying…"

"I'm saying I want us to live our lives in the bedroom in a Dom/sub world, but we can't go back to how we were."

He threaded his hands through my hair. My head tingled from the arousal his touch created. I hadn't been this excited in a while.

"Let me do some serious thinking and come up with something. Then we'll have a talk."

With his hands still tangled in my mass of crazy curls, he kissed me. His tongue probed deep, and my own scrambled to meet his demands.

****

I love how I fit so perfectly under his chin. Once I started the story, the words rolled from my mouth with ease. Not seeing him gave me the courage to go back in time. I paused, noticing our breathing merged into one breath. Our chests both rose and fell with the same rhythm. The hum of the furnace and suite's refrigerator rumbled from another room.

"You know," he said, "when you said to me you'd lose your nerve if you didn't tell me right then…I was so certain you were about to ask for a divorce. I could hardly stand waiting for those words to come out of your mouth."

I almost turned to face him but stopped. Laying my head against his solid and warm chest was so much better. "Why didn't you tell me?"

A chuckle rumbled deep in his chest. "I didn't want to give you any ideas."

"You want me to go on?"

"Every word."

Chapter Twenty

I had good news.

I undressed Jordan as soon as he stepped in the door from work. I wasn't ripping his clothes off for sex. Because he said he wanted to change first, I wanted him into jeans and a T-shirt now. He also had news, he said.

"So what is your big news?" he said after pulling the Miami of Ohio University T-shirt over his head.

"I got a job. Well not so much a real job, but work. I have some work."

"Great, but what do you mean?"

I bounced on our bed and scooted to the headboard. "I ran into David Sutter at Koffee's, and he told me he wasn't happy with how his last two manuscripts were edited."

"Who did them?" Jordan joined me on the bed, but kept a distance so we could talk upright.

"I did his first two, but my boss took the last two from me and gave him to Lori Mays. I hate to use the word *hate*, but I hate her. Anyway, he asked if I would consider editing his new manuscript. He's no longer under contract to the company and is going independent."

"I'm happy for you. You need this." Jordan collected my hand and kissed my palm. "Maybe doing this can get you some other work."

"This is the best part." His kissing my palm made

my heart flutter like the first time we kissed. "David is pretty well-known, and he has several author friends. I told him if he refers anyone to me, I will give him a thirty percent discount on his next manuscript. He said he has lots of people he can send to me."

I stuck my face within inches of Jordan's nose. "I have a job," I whispered.

He grabbed me, threw me to the mattress, and held my wrists above my head. The act triggered a memory, and I caught my breath. "What are you doing to me…Sir?"

Jordan moaned, and then crushed his lips to mine. "I'm going to fuck you until you pass out. Then I'm going to wake you up and fuck you all over again." He caressed my cheek with tongue. "Because you haven't been this happy in months."

"I thought you had something to tell me?"

"It can wait."

****

I think I did pass out. Whatever the case, I hadn't had an orgasm so intense since he used the leather gloves.

In my haze of a mind-blowing fuck, the skin on the back of my neck burned hot. Jordan was blowing his hot breath just under my hairline. "Wake up, Angel. I want to discuss something."

I rolled over to my side exposing my breasts and stilled aroused nipples. "Here, sit up, next to me."

As soon as I snuggled close, he stretched his arm over the side of the bed, retrieving a piece of paper from his suit pants puddled in a heap on the floor.

"I've been thinking about our conversation, and I don't want to give up the kink with you. I could live without it, but not without you. You, Angel, are my dream, my life, and when you give yourself to me wholly, I feel like the luckiest guy on the planet. I don't feel like something is missing."

He unfolded the paper and scanned the contents. "That being said, if we want to continue this lifestyle, we have to have defined roles and rules. Because we didn't, which caused some of our problems." With the back of his hand, Jordan brushed my cheek with his knuckles. "Let me read this to you, and you tell me if you are okay with what I've come up with."

I nodded and waited for a new door to open. Somehow, I never connected BDSM with formality. I didn't embrace the life with a seriousness, and I should have.

Jordan's deep breathing possessed a ragged edge.

He was nervous. This man so confident in his career, perused the paper he clutched with hands unable to hide the slight tremble.

"If you want to continue, we have to make changes. We cannot go on as we were because we were a miserable kink failure. Which is my fault. I've been too vague because I admit, I was a little scared to get back into the lifestyle, but I so wanted to with you.

"This is how we will have to be. There will be what I'm calling locked sessions, meaning the collar you wear will be locked. This will signal we are in a session and the rules will apply. In order for this to work, we have to have set rules and consequences for breaking rules so there will be no confusion."

I could see the list, but he read aloud each one to me.

During locked sessions, you will obey what I say,

no hesitations or questions or refusals unless you safeword. Failure to do so will lead to repercussions.

We will use safewords.

During locked sessions, you will be given choices and you must choose or you get nothing.

During locked sessions, you will not speak freely unless I give you permission.

During locked sessions, you will address me as "Sir."

The length of time of locked sessions are at my discretion, but if I ask your opinion, I expect an honest answer.

There will be no repercussions for safewording. I want you safe, happy and trusting me to have your best interests always in my thoughts.

I determine discipline and I will not tell you how much or how long it will last.

I determine everything we do in our locked sessions, unless I specifically ask you. (Won't happen very often.)

At every moment during locked sessions and any other time, you are never to doubt I love you deeply.

Either of us can end this contract at any time.

"May I add something?

I scribbled my request on the list. *Will you use a flogger on me?*

"Angel?" he said when he read my question. "I…"

"Jordan. I know you don't want to hurt me, but you won't. I know you won't."

He scribbled his answer under my question. "*Under consideration. Will be determined later.*"

Well it wasn't a "no." So I was a little hopeful and nervous at my boldness. "One more thing. I understand all of this about the locked sessions and what they mean, but... Could I? I mean I really miss wearing my connection to you. I miss wearing the collar." Wow. Those words sounded weird coming from my mouth. Never in my life had I considered a phrase with those words, and here I was requesting my husband to let me put a strap of leather back on my neck. I missed the pressure of the band, and how my body reacted to its placement.

"I've thought about that, too." He opened the drawer next to the bed and pulled out two items. The one I could see was another smooth black leather collar, but different—barely a half an inch wide. I examined the piece resting in his hand and fondled the pliable leather.

"It's smaller I know, but I just think this one is better suited for you, and the other one you were wearing we will use sometimes for locked sessions."

"Okay," I couldn't wait until he adjusted the new collar to my neck. In fact, I was already getting tingly in my tingler spot.

He handed me the other item in a three-inch square box. I lifted the lid to find a thin black leather cord with a tiny silver latching clasp. A small silver disk pendant sat on the end of the cord. I removed the cord from the box, turning over the pendant to see the *My Angel* inscription on the back.

"On days you don't want to cover up," he said. "Like the silver one, but for casual wearing. No one would know what this is."

"It's very simple, and I love it." Although I did love the message and couldn't wait to wear the new proclamation—right now I wanted the exquisite pressure of the other collar pressing against my neck. I handed Jordan the thin black one. "Now?" I asked.

I lifted my hair as he fastened the collar around my neck. The sensation had me burning already.

"Are we going to have to break this in?" he teased.

"Maybe." I wasn't teasing.

His light-hearted face turned serious. "This doesn't change. Only me will put this on or take it off of you."

For one of the few times in my life, I had no words. I bit my lip and nodded.

I had one more question, a very frightening one. "What if we end this again, this lifestyle? What happens to us?"

He sat silent for a moment before cupping my face with his hands. His thumb caressed my cheek, and I could see moisture in his eyes. "Nothing, Angel. Nothing will happen. We will live a vanilla life, but better. Nothing will change how I feel about you. I love you."

Chapter Twenty-One

The Friday following the reestablishment of our agreement, I began work on David Sutter's manuscript. I loved his story about testing the faith of a group of teenagers lost on a hiking trip. So engrossed, I failed to hear Jordan enter the condo.

When he peeked his head through the door of the second bedroom, I jumped from the intrusion in my mind. "Hi. You startled me."

"Getting involved in your work?"

I smiled and stretched aching shoulder muscles. "Yes, feels so good."

He stepped into the room and leaned against the doorframe. "I have something to make you feel good if you're interested."

His eyes sparkled with mischief, and oh my God, the smile rocking his face had me wanting to launch myself from the bed. But, no, I played cool. "I might be interested."

Jordan approached with his right fist closed. He leaned down to me, placed his hand behind my neck, and kissed me. A faint click sent ecstatic chills through me.

He broke the kiss and said. "We are now in a locked session. If you need me to slow, tell me 'yellow.' If we need to stop, tell me 'red,' and everything stops. Can you do that?"

My hand went to the back of my neck, and I touched the small padlock dangling from a metal loop. The lock was little more than what you would use for a piece of luggage, but this tiny piece of metal would change our relationship once again. Mentally, I reread the list of rules Jordan wrote and I agreed to. "Yes…Sir. I can do everything on the list."

Just saying those words sent pulses of anticipation, joy and a little bit of fear through my body.

Jordan held out his hand to me. "Go to our room and get undressed. Wait on the edge of the bed for me."

I accepted his hand and forced my trembling body to stand. His touch warmed the sudden chill encompassing my body. I nodded.

"Words, Angel."

"Yes, Sir." Again, using the word 'Sir,' in reference to my husband didn't make me feel less. No, quite the opposite. By following his instructions, I would be the one with the power. Once simple word, and I could stop everything.

Huge mental slap. I had the power all along, but I was too busy fighting for rights I owned from the start.

I left the room, and when I cleared his line of sight, I sprinted for our bedroom, stripping off my clothes in a frenzy. Rushing into our bathroom, I swigged a bit of mouthwash and choked when a drop escaped down my throat. *Calm down.*

Who was I kidding? I couldn't calm down. This…this unknown was killing me. I pulled my hair from the clip on my head and the stacked mess of dark brown curls tumbled and bounced across my shoulders. A spritz of my favorite orange-scented perfume, and I was ready to be ravaged by the most gorgeous and sweetest man I'd ever known.

As per orders, I made my way to the edge of bed and sat and waited and waited. I could hear Jordan speaking in a low voice, but I couldn't tell if he were on the phone or if someone was at the door. "Go away," I wanted to yell through the door to the unwanted intruder on my happy time.

But I didn't. I'm sure yelling through the door was a punishable deed.

Punishment.

Now my mind swirled with a list of what were punishable offenses and what would punishment entail. Jordan wasn't into spanking or whipping, so that was off the table. He said he didn't like the act and would never use one on a woman. After witnessing the little demo of the flogging and whipping at the party, I just might like a little flick to the butt.

I stared at my wedding ring set, watching the light dance through the prism of the gems. I never allowed them from my hand. Nude, with nothing adorning me but my diamond, I chuckled. I used to feel self-conscientious about being naked, but Jordan's worship-like treatment of my body gave me confidence. Far from perfect, but he sucked the fleshy parts and worked the muscled parts like a coach. He once told me he would tie me out on the lawn of the state capital building and fuck me there, if I would let him. Yeah, no. I had my own set of rules, and he had a career we needed to pay the mortgage.

Again, so lost in the plate of spaghetti posing as my brain, I didn't hear Jordan enter the room.

"Angel. Are you ready for me?

"Yes, Sir."

He stalked to me and dropped to his knees, wrapping his arms around my waist. He nibbled at the fleshy part of my stomach. "You're so beautiful, Angel. I could taste you forever."

Keep licking and we won't need to do anything else.

"Stand for me."

As I stood, Jordan revealed the black silk ropes from his jeans back pocket. Swallowing hard, I always had one moment of panic just before he bound my hands.

I started to turn around so he could bind me. "No. Stay facing me," he said in a low and smooth tone.

I presented my wrists, and his slow and sure hands bound the rope around my wrists. The sensation of the tightening of the bindings almost made me giddy at our return to kink.

When he finished, he drew my hands to my lips as he caressed my knuckles with his own mouth.

With precise motion, he unbuttoned his shirt, revealing his muscled chest that veed to his waist. I never envisioned men being beautiful, just handsome, but dear God, he was beautiful, with the way the low light reflected the olive of his skin and rich chocolate of his hair.

"Now, I want you to place your arms around my neck."

He lowered his body enough where I could loop my bound wrists around the back of his neck. He stepped three steps away from the bed, taking me with him. "I have a treat for you. You'll watch only me. No matter what. If you turn your head, not only will we stop, but you will be punished." He tipped my chin to face commanding eyes. "Understand?"

I nodded. He glared.

"Yes, Sir, I understand."

Jordan's gaze left me for the doorway of our bedroom. I kept my eyes focused on his face, but even in the silence, I sensed a person in the room. I detected a scent not belonging to my husband, but the scent was neither masculine nor feminine, nor familiar.

What in the hell was happening?

When the strings of leather whispered across my shoulders, the resolve to keep from peeing myself almost choked. *A flogger!* With every stroke, I shivered from the sensation of the leather nipping my skin. I didn't feel pain, but rather a deep-rooted gratification bubbling inside.

The person wielding the instrument crisscrossed my backside to my thighs with a growing intensity. *Whack!* I drew a sharp breath when something wider struck my butt cheek stinging more than a little. Then the swishing of the flogger returned, again followed by another sharp slap to my ass. The burning pain transformed into arousal, and I closed my eyes remembering the party and the manifestation of shear serenity on the face of Laura while she yielded to the strap.

"Angel, open your eyes," Jordan commanded. The muscles in his neck tensed, and his breathing increased.

I responded and smiled, but the smile turned to "ouch," when the crop struck the side of my breast. Repeatedly, the leather slapped my skin. Harder and harder, the crop landed on my backside. I trembled from the pain, but yet, I loved the conscientiousness of the arousal in my soul and body. Every pore, every hair tingled with awareness.

When I believed I was at the very edge of my threshold, the soft fluttering of the flogger returned. After several more strokes, Jordan acknowledged the mystery person, and the motion stopped. The soft clicking of the door told me the deliverer of the strikes left the room, leaving the two of us alone in our world.

I didn't realize I was breathing so haphazardly, until Jordan told me take a few deep breaths. "Are you all right?" he asked running his fingers through my hair.

"Very much so." *Holy fuck*. And to think as a kid, I ran from my dad when the belt whipped out. Indeed, a different situation, but I wondered what the belt could do now. Now that Jordan had a flogger proxy, maybe I would find out sometime.

"I couldn't do this to you, but when you watched the demo, the look on your face was so dreamlike, and I conceded you had to have the experience."

"Who was that?"

"A secret always to remain a secret." Not what I wanted to hear. Not knowing who's doing something to you is weird. This person had to be someone Jordan trusted with his life.

He bent again, removing my wrists from his neck. "Shall we continue on our own?"

In my stinging euphoria, Jordan guided me to the middle of the bed and raised my wrists high over my head, attaching the binding to another rope with a clip on the end. His hands grasped my waist as he skimmed his body along my torso. Little currents of electricity sparked into my blood with every touch of his tongue. His mouth aligned with my entrance as he squeezed my butt with his powerful hands. So much so, my ass stung from the cut of his nails.

Every time I wiggled, the virgin skin on my back burned from the lashes, and the sheets I once believed soft, scratched like sandpaper.

He licked a jagged line up my inner thigh before nipping the tender skin with his teeth. Each bite progressed to a sharper level. In the morning, I would bear the delicious purple color of his marking and check the mirror to admire his work.

When he paused at my gate, I held my breath. I didn't know which appendage I cherished more—his magic dick or his magic tongue, but right now, the one was about to torture me would be my favorite until he used the other.

****

The locked session lasted through the night until after I cooked breakfast for us the next morning. I didn't notice before, but the key to the tiny padlock lay in full view on my dresser, signaling to me that I still held the power.

I loved our new relationship. With the clear rules and expectations, I relaxed and Jordan was more confidant in his handling of our sessions. What hadn't happened yet was any discipline, but all was about to change.

Chapter Twenty-Two

"I think we're getting to the good part," Jordan said. He buried his face in my hair, kissing my scalp. And while I loved what he was doing, I couldn't help but think "Eww, at the sweat still dribbling down my neck. The more of the story I told, the hotter I got and where our skin touched, sticky hot sweat joined us.

"I think I'm getting to the embarrassing part. Do I have to continue? You know what happened. You designed the whole thing."

My ass shifted from his hand rummaging through his front pocket. In his palm sat the tiny padlock. "I'm giving you a choice. You can willingly *embarrass* yourself—although I think you were beautiful—or I can order you to describe our first discipline session. Either way, you should never be ashamed."

"I can't say I'm ashamed much. When I think about what you did, I get all wound up in my puss."

He tossed the lock onto the nightstand. "I will happily unwind your puss when you finish my bedtime story."

****

At the very beginning of our marriage, Jordan said he wanted our Saturday mornings to be just us—no outside intrusions, which I understood to mean anything work related as well.

Our locked session began on a Friday after Jordan

used a half-day vacation and was still in effect as I cooked pancakes and sausage for breakfast Saturday morning. My leg and arm muscles ached from the bindings last night, but the soreness reminded me more of a good workout rather than a night of bound passion.

When I walked into our bedroom to tell Jordan breakfast was ready, my jaw dropped. He sat on the bed, engrossed in whatever file open on his laptop.

"Jordan, breakfast."

He never lost focus. "Sure. I just need to finish this."

What? This was Saturday morning. I always adhered to the *no intrusions* rule.

"Jordan, this is Saturday, and *your* breakfast is ready."

"And I said I need to finish something."

In my head, I heard my dad saying, "Don't use that tone with me."

My hands planted on my hips in frustration. "Your rule, Jordan. I made your breakfast as *you* requested."

"And you don't question me during this time."

Oh, shit. I'm done. My brain throbbed with pissed off heat. I stomped into the kitchen, swiped his plate piled high with steaming homemade pancakes and sausage, and threw the plate into the trash.

I stomped into the bedroom and changed from my robe into running pants and a black quarter zip top.

Now, I had his attention.

"What are you doing?" He enunciated every word. The commander-in-chief tone only pissed me off.

"I'm going out."

"No, you're not."

"Watch me."

"Angel!" My blood froze from his dark voice, but I ignored all the signs forewarning punishment. The rising temperature of my own ire thawed anything keeping me in the same room.

I slipped on running shoes, zipped the shirt all the way up to hide the collar and left the condo.

When I stepped onto the canal walk, I broke into a jog. After five minutes, I remembered how much I hated running and the calendar read August. August is a synonym for miserable in Indiana. Black long-sleeved high neck athletic shirt. Good choice. Being pissed off altered the sensible choice part of my brain, but I kept running. I followed the rules. I loved the rules, and the one who made the rules was breaking them. However, I had an inkling if I stopped running, I would be the one in trouble.

Dripping with sweat and exhaustion from my less than a mile run, I collapsed on the same grassy hill where I hit Jordan in the head with my phone. My history with this deceivingly beautiful spot was less than stellar.

A dark shadow loomed over me. I opened my eyes but shielded them from the sun. Outlined by the bright sun and cloudless sky, my jailer had tracked me down. My escaped short-lived, and punishment imminent.

He sat beside me and offered nothing—no water, not even help sitting up.

"Something you want to discuss?"

Anyone walking by would see an attractive relaxed man chewing on a blade of grass, but the evil lurking behind the calm façade unnerved me. If ever there were a time I wished to rewind the two minutes before flying out the door, it was now.

Rivers of sweat ran through my hair, trickling into the shirt and collar making me start to itch. A salty bead dripped from my nose. I wiped and sniffed—not my most attractive moment. When I'd stopped running, the overwhelming heat and humidity threatened to consume me. I desperately wanted to take off the shirt, but I couldn't.

"I guess I'm a little confused and angry." In reality, I was seething, but I played coy and smiled through each word.

"Go on." His icy blues were not amused with my behavior.

"You said Saturday mornings were us time, and no outside interference. I fixed the breakfast *you* wanted, and you wouldn't come to eat because *you* were too busy on your fuckin' laptop." I swallowed hard. "I meant stupid laptop."

"I needed to respond to that particular e-mail as soon as possible. Several thousand dollars important." His intense stare unnerved me. No way was I going to win this argument, but still…

"You couldn't have waited until after breakfast and at least mentioned you needed to do something work related?"

"Are you forgetting the part of our agreement said there was to be no questioning what I'm doing?"

This just might be my loophole. "I understood the questioning thing was just about sex and kink."

Damn. Stop looking at me with those icy eyes. You're gonna blind me.

"Did I say our agreement only pertained to sex and kink?"

Fuck! Checkmate. "No…sir."

"What are we going to do now?" He stood and clamped down my hand. With a strong grip, he hauled me close, and I almost fell into his chest, but he stopped me before I had any chance of connecting and trying to make nice.

"I'm going to go home, shower, and make you a new breakfast?"

"Wrong."

"I don't understand."

He raked his fingers through my sweaty hair. "Ew," he said, wiping the moisture on my top. "We're going home. You'll make me a new breakfast, and then if I allow, you may shower. Then we'll have our first discipline session."

Although I contemplated silliness of this scenario—I'm an adult and facing punishment, but something about the low velvety tone of his voice telling me so, hotwired my libido.

The round one mess of the breakfast prep remained on the counter. I rinsed the bowl, measured more ingredients, and put more sausage into a skillet. Once finished, I arranged the food on the plate and added an orange slice for decoration. Give me points for effort.

I set the plate in front of Jordan as he sat at our dining table. He examined the plate until a devious smile swept across his face. "You have until I finish eating to be showered and be standing here or I will extend your punishment."

"How long?"

He lifted the fork to cut a bite of sausage. "I don't know, so you better not dawdle."

Before "How is that fair?" left my lips, I fled to the bathroom.

Huffing and puffing my way back to the table, my hair was still too wet, and all I managed to don was my robe, but when I skidded to a halt, Jordan still had two bites of pancakes left and half a mug of coffee.

"Made it."

"No talking." He sipped the coffee before perusing my presence.

Of all the rules set forth, *no talking* was definitely the most challenging.

"Go put on your tall boots and return to me minus the robe."

"Just the boots. My hooker boots?"

"Are you suddenly hard of hearing?"

I sighed. "No, Sir." I turned to retrieve the over the knee stiletto boots my husband's dick loved. Uncomfortable as hell, but whatever.

As elegantly as a naked, hooker-booted woman could, I returned to the sovereign of my destiny.

He'd abandoned me.

So I believed.

I stood staring straight ahead, remaining quiet, and listening to his bare feet pad across the floor. A cool breeze touched my neck when he lifted my hair from my shoulders and snapped an industrial size clip in the hair piled high on top of my head.

Then I saw it.

A different collar. One I'd never seen.

Jordan undid the lock on my current collar, unfastened the buckle, and slid my security from my neck to put in place a very unfamiliar one. Instinctively, I lifted my chin. This collar's proportions were much different. Though still some sort of fake leather, the width had to be at least two inches wide.

He deliberately slowed the process of fitting the collar, raising my anxiety level to high alert. *I would not panic. I would not panic. I can stop this anytime.* I refused to call *uncle* the first time through a discipline session.

Once he fastened the catch and snapped the familiar click of the padlock, I swallowed hard—my throat uniting with the leather. Yeah. This was a little uncomfortable, but not unbearable. The width made lowering my chin awkward.

Wasn't sure I cared for this. So punishment was indeed going to be punishment.

Jordan kissed my ear and whispered. "Can you do this?"

"Yes," I whispered back. *I'm no quitter. I may not like it, but I'll be damned if I safeword out of this one.*

To my surprise, Jordan wasn't finished adorning me with discipline. I began chewing my lip when he approached, ball gag in hand. When the ball touched my lips, I cemented them shut.

"Open your mouth, Angel," he commanded.

I hesitated. "Why?"

"Hmm. Maybe because you have trouble with too much talking." He pressed the ball harder against my lips. "Open."

Closing my eyes, I opened my mouth, allowing him to insert the gag. As he tightened the straps, he said. "You remember your safeword?"

How in the fuck could I safeword?

I nodded as far as the collar allowed. I may rethink the safeword thing.

"Just raise your hand if you need to."

Once the gag was in place, an immediate need to

swallow gripped me. Nothing was wrong. I wasn't hurting or in danger. He warm lips touched my ear, sending a tickle throughout my body. "That's my Angel."

I didn't know what to do, so I remained motionless with my hands clasped in front of me. I stopped swallowing and accepted the new consciousness.

Jordan retrieved his empty plate from the table and rang the opening bell on discipline. "You're going to clean the kitchen while I get some work done."

He smirked at my still-standing-in-the-same-place body. "And the longer you take, the longer this will continue.

Oh, so when I finish cleaning, he'll undo all of this? Sweet.

I snatched away the plate to commence cleaning the mess I made earlier. The collar and gag made for a troublesome effort. I had trouble seeing anything beneath me and saliva kept dripping from my mouth so I continually had to wipe the spit from the sink, counter, and clean dishes.

Once I finished, I joined Jordan sitting at the table.

"I didn't tell you to sit." He lifted his gaze from the laptop—a stern exterior clouded his handsome features. "Go stand behind the sofa...and don't lean."

By now, the boots were hurting my feet, drool ran like a rabid dog, and I was damn sure I'd learned my lesson.

Where instructed, I stood arrow straight. I ground my teeth so tight, my jaw ached—all to keep myself from scowling at my husband typing away on important mission I'm now paying the price for questioning its validity.

I could raise my hand and end all of this, but in reality, I was getting a little horny from the inability to speak or even sway. I clenched hard so my arousal didn't drip down my leg.

After minutes, hours, or could even have been days, Jordan closed the laptop and stood before me. He wiped my drool with his tongue.

My chest heaved, and I wanted nothing more than to taste him.

He dispatched a quick hand behind me, releasing the gag. I worked the stiffness from my jaw.

He held the gag in his hand just high enough I could see the wet ball. "Now, I'll give you a choice. You can either wear this for a while longer and be done, or you can take me in your mouth and continue."

I dropped to the floor so fast I worried I'd shattered my kneecaps.

****

When Jordan said we would continue after he pumped my mouth long and hard, I misunderstood what he meant.

He meant, he reinserted the gag, trussed me up from the top rail running across the foot of our bed, and propelled my body to the edge of climax and stopped...three times, all while I still wore the hooker boots.

Once he released my arms and the gag, I collapsed into his. My legs could hold me no more.

Oh, but we weren't finished. He told me to dress in the corset and black miniskirt. He allowed me a different pair of boots, ones with a lower, thicker heel. I still wore the uncomfortable collar, and my nerves batted at my body because I had a feeling we were leaving the safety of the condo.

Jordan handed me my short leather jacket. *For god's sake, it's August.* I shrugged the thing on, zipped up enough to conceal the collar, and pushed the sleeves up as far as I could.

We left and walked outside in the heat to the bus stop. Jordan handed me a pair of sunglasses. "Put these on."

I slipped on the glasses and my world fell dark. He had covered the inside of the glasses with black tape, and I could only get a hint of daytime streaming from the bottom of the lens. In my darkness, my ears filled with the gearing from the approaching of a city bus and whoosh from the hydraulics when the door opened.

Jordan held my hand, guiding me up the steps of the bus, while he dropped coins one by one in the metal and told the driver hello like he possessed all the time in the world.

I lost concept of time as we rode around the city. The cool air blowing in the bus kept me comfortable, and Jordan's protective arm around my shoulder calmed my fear of this very public punishment.

"We're getting off here," He leaned into me, talking in a low voice. "Hold onto my hand, you'll be fine.

Once we stepped from the bus, I could sense the feel of the approaching evening because the morning session extended well into the afternoon. The air temperature had cooled a bit, but humidity still lingered keeping me sweating beneath my jacket. The partnering of leather and sweat was not going to smell of flowers later.

Jordan became my seeing-eye person, as I had no

idea where we were. We walked on sidewalks, crossed busy streets, and made our way through grassy areas of downtown. Even though I couldn't see, surely we'd been gone long enough the sun had to be near setting.

Though the night air cooled a few degrees, I sweated profusely from wearing the jacket, but no way in hell would I ask to expose my secret.

I heard voices and sounds of the city...cars, sirens, horns, but nothing was familiar.

Jordan stopped walking, the pace keeping me clacking the boots on the cement. He changed speed and direction, and I welcomed the respite. My boots squished the ground beneath me, while the air hung heavy with the perfume of evergreen. He ordered me to sit, and I slowly lowered myself to the ground, as blades of summer stressed grass scratched my legs. Still unaware of my surroundings, I wanted to rip off the glasses, but since Jordan didn't say I could, I was trying to behave and not to extend my punishment, because right now, I was hot, sticky, scratchy and a few other choice adjectives.

He unzipped and nudged my jacket from my shoulders until I was able to free my arms from the sleeves. The relief I embraced from the air touching and cooling my sweaty skin was short-lived because now, the collar was visible.

I wanted nothing more than to end this. I wasn't into exhibitionism not a teeny bit.

"Remember when I said I wanted to lay you out on the capitol lawn?" His breath blew hot on my face as he helped my back to the ground. The grass tickled my exposed shoulders.

"Jordan, please. Don't make me do this?"

"Say the word, Angel."

I didn't want to safeword out of this, but his fantasy catapulted my limits to the fringe of breakdown. Heavy and rapid breaths attacked my conscientiousness.

His knuckles brushed my cheek, and I detected the voices of people nearby. What were they seeing and how soon would I hear sirens approaching? Who would bail us out of jail?

His hand descended on the top of my breasts ready to spill from the corset. He began circling his fingers and kissing the hollow between my breasts. His hand brushed the corset.

Wait. Wait. Wait.

I remembered an earlier conversation.

When we were going to the kink party, Jordan wouldn't let me wear the corset. *For his eyes only,* he said.

Wherever we were, no one could see us. I yanked the sunglasses from my face to assess my surroundings—outside, but not exposed on the capital lawn, as was my biggest nightmare. A dense copse of spruce trees and bayberry bushes shielded us from the public, but I could hear voices engaged in every day conversations—not "Holy crap look at those crazy people having sex in the middle of the city. Someone call the police."

Now I understood mind fucking. Not a fan.

When I procured the ability to breathe without hyperventilating, I palmed his cheek. His tender and broad smile erased any fear of him carrying out what I perceived.

"How did you know?" He wiped the not attractive

perspiration from my forehead.

I ran my hand across the corset. "This. Finally dawned on me you said this was for your eyes only. So why would you have me wear the very item you didn't want people see? I don't know where we are, but this isn't exactly public."

Jordan lay beside me with his hand across my belly. "There's a rather hidden and little known park behind my office. I come here sometimes to get away from my desk and to dream about taking you right here."

I raised on my elbow to face him. "Punishment over?"

"Punishment over." He pulled me on top and slipped a hand between my legs "Unless you'd consider...

I pinched his cheek. "I'm going to teeter on a disciplinary ledge here, but that's not only a 'no,' but a hell no."

Chapter Twenty-Three

"So there's my story, in my own words, Mr. Caldera." I flipped over like a fish and straddled his waist. I walked my fingers up his chest to his nipples, and with each circle of my fingertip, he tensed. Powerful little tool I have.

"Why are you smiling?" I melted into his embrace.

"I think I needed to hear your story. Trying to keep up with how your mind works is daunting to say the least. So thank you for giving me a little bit of insight.

A knock sounded on the door.

"Did you order room service?" My head jerked toward the sound of the invasion of my plans.

Jordan looked at his watch. "No. Well, not until much later, when I planned to get you drunk and fuck your brains out all night until wee in the morning."

"I don't have to be drunk. I'm always up for a good fucking." I pulled from his grasp. Jordan double-checked his watch. "Maybe it's Jessica. She might have another question." I said.

I shrugged into Jordan's T-shirt and ran to answer the door.

"Did you forget…"

Sabrina. Oh my God. Sabrina.

"I was waiting in the lobby and Jessica Forner walks by over to some guy also sitting there. Was she the one who was interviewing you?"

My best friend hadn't talked to me in months, and I get no "Hello, I missed you," or even a "kiss my ass." Or better yet, "I'm here because…"

A murky fog of confusion surrounded my brain. Stunned was the only adjective I had. What was she doing here? "Uh, yes that was her."

Sabrina marched her way into the suite. "Girl, you know I don't talk this way, but you're fucked."

Anna Hague

About the Author

My career in Sports Journalism spans over twenty-five years. I currently do freelance sports reporting to allow more time for romance writing. I published my debut contemporary novel Captured Hearts in November of 2016. I live in central Indiana with my husband, three parrots, and a dog.

~*~

Visit Anna at

http://annahague.com

~*~

To chat with Anna Hague and other Wild Rose Press authors of erotic romance, join us at

www.groups.yahoo.com/group/thewilderroses.

Also Available from
The Wild Rose Press, Inc. and other retailers

Play a Game with Me
Games People Play Book One
By Cadence Vonn

Maximilian Westfield has resurrected his family's company under the controlling eye of the major shareholder–his mother. To keep the company, he must marry the woman she chooses, no matter how inane or spineless. He is resigned to go through with the arranged marriage until he meets a feisty costume designer who will never meet his mother's standards. A stolen kiss spurs his lustful cravings. Once he tastes the spirited beauty's charms, he knows he has to find a way to keep her and his company. No other woman will do.

The daughter of a powerful British businessman, Teresa Medici Staffordshire leads her life as Tess Medici to avoid men out to please her father. Then she meets Maximilian, a sexy uptight CEO. From the moment he unleashes his expert fingers on her skin, she's hooked. His erotic games make her body hum with pleasure. Determined to lure Max out to play, every encounter becomes a game of enticement. But his commitment to his family business and his mother's determination to marry him off makes it impossible to take the relationship public, and Tess refuses to be his guilty little secret.

Choices become consequences, their future is on the line, and Max and Tess are running out of time.

Mr. OH

Billionaire Doms Book One

By Vonnie Davis

He doesn't do emotions...She's all about them.

Dental hygienist by day and a tattoo artist by night, Jazmine "Jazz" Archer is known for her penchant for flair and her sassy attitude. She estimates her wealth by her beloved family and friends. When a cancelled flight leaves her stuck at a hotel with a super-stuffy but outrageously gorgeous businessman who threatens her with a spanking, she's surprised to realize the submissive she suppressed so long ago is begging her to take him up on his offer.

Self-made billionaire Blake O'Hearn is as conservative as they come. He sure as hell shouldn't be attracted to the flamboyant female with voluptuous curves and curls that dance when she talks. But behind her bold manner lies a submissive crying for attention, and the Dom in him aches to give it to her. The only thing he can't give her is love.